THIS SKIN WAS ONCE MINE and

"Eric LaRocca's distinctive literary voice is a welcome addition to queer horror. I look forward to seeing his legacy grow."

Poppy Z. Brite, author of *Exquisite Corpse*

"Eric LaRocca keeps getting better. Grotesque, heartbreaking, and deeply unsettling, this is the kind of transgressive horror that exposes the vulnerable human heart, that reminds us of our shared pain. Just the byline on his work—'by Eric LaRocca'—should be considered a trigger warning. You know going in that it's going to hurt. Caveat lector."

Christopher Golden, author of *The House of Last Resort* and *Road of Bones*

"Eric LaRocca is a singular talent, who writes ruthlessly, beautifully, bravely about brutality, who challenges readers to find their humanity, and ultimately hope, in the face of such horrors."

Rachel Harrison, author of *The Return* and *Black Sheep*

"Eric LaRocca distorts spaces, both internal and external, creating new cavities within our bodies, fresh chasms in our minds, and flooding them with nothing but absolute terror. *This Skin Was Once Mine and Other Disturbances* makes for exquisite suffering and confirms LaRocca's mantle as the heir apparent to Clive Barker and Poppy Z. Brite. Glory be to the new king of horror."

Clay McLeod Chapman, author of *What Kind of Mother* and *Ghost Eaters*

"A twisty, intricate gathering of bleak fates. Beneath the skin of delicate prose lies indelicate menace. Eric LaRocca has penned a book that's obsessively captivating, wherein even hope hurts like a shard of glass."

Hailey Piper, Bram Stoker Award®-winning author of *Queen of Teeth*

"An intense collection that stalks its way around the kinship between pleasure and pain. LaRocca's tremendous empathy allows him to look unblinkingly at the dark corners that others turn away from, in a way that makes his horror not only devastating but heartbreaking."

Brian Evenson, author of *The Glassy, Burning Floor of Hell*

"These raw and brilliant stories lure you in and then slice you to the core. Their terrors and scars will persist. Cutting, insightful horror from a new master."

Tim Lebbon, author of *The Silence* and *Among the Living*

THIS
SKIN WAS
ONCE MINE
AND OTHER
DISTURBANCES

ERIC LaROCCA

THIS
SKIN WAS
ONCE MINE

AND OTHER
DISTURBANCES

TITAN BOOKS

This Skin Was Once Mine and Other Disturbances
Hardback edition ISBN: 9781803366647
Paperback edition ISBN: 9781803366661
E-book edition ISBN: 9781803366654

Published by Titan Books
A division of Titan Publishing Group Ltd
144 Southwark Street, London SE1 0UP

This edition: April 2025
1 3 5 7 9 10 8 6 4 2

A CIP catalogue record for this title is available
from the British Library.

Printed and bound by
CPI Group (UK) Ltd, Croydon, CR0 4YY.

Dear reader,

Thank you for your care and consideration while approaching *This Skin Was Once Mine and Other Disturbances.*

I wrote these four tales over the span of two years while I was overwhelmed with thoughts about the dynamics of certain relationships—specifically the ways in which we inherently harm one another and the obsessions we nurture to prevent further suffering. It should be obvious to note that all the stories collected here deal with human pain and trauma in some form or another.

Though you may already be familiar with my writing prior to opening this book, I wholeheartedly encourage you to check in with yourself before carrying on. I've been prompted by my editor to warn you that this book includes graphic depictions of child abuse and self-harm. Each story is intensely claustrophobic as well. I expect these elements will be distressing for some readers, so I heartily suggest you sincerely consider whether or not you'd like to subject yourself to such upsetting material.

Before you press onward, please take a moment to put down this book and truly consider how you'd like to proceed. Go for a walk. Listen to music. Make a cup of tea. Please consider this a final warning before you begin.

Regardless of your decision, thank you for approaching this collection with such attention and thoughtfulness.

Eric LaRocca

October 2023, Boston, MA

For Paul Tremblay
A devoted friend and a fearless writer

"Through indiscriminate suffering men know fear and fear is the most divine emotion. It is the stones for altars and the beginning of wisdom. Half gods are worshipped in wine and flowers. Real gods require blood."

Zora Neale Hurston

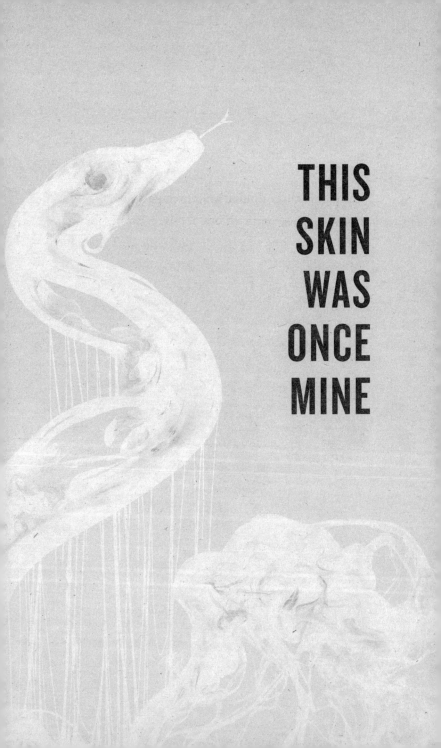

THIS
SKIN
WAS
ONCE
MINE

"The past is never dead. It's not even past."

William Faulkner

OCTOBER 25, 2021

The worst thing a person can do to you after they've hurt you is let you live.

That's how you truly and unmistakably destroy another human being.

I say this with some authority on the matter. While many might reason that the greatest cruelty of all would be to offer hope to someone who clearly has none, I would instead argue that the gift of survival after unspeakable trauma is a much more excruciating fortune.

There's nothing romantic, nothing decidedly empowering about becoming a survivor. Of course, television has played a significant role in our cultural perception of survivors as strong, unbeatable, and almost divine pillars of integrity. We fawn over the image of the bald child who's receiving their last dose of chemotherapy. We praise the sight of the blood-soaked high-schooler who crawled across a pile of dead classmates and made their way to safety.

Naturally, there's an audience for anything and everything.

People will always be drawn to the idea of someone succeeding and becoming something truly glorious after they've been ravaged, defiled, very nearly obliterated. But I can assure you there's nothing magnificent or outstanding about it. It is no rare, distinguished gift to survive tragedy, disaster, misfortune.

Nobody talks about the quiet, unbearable moments when the cameras aren't rolling, when the interviewers aren't shoving microphones in your face and asking you, "What does it feel like?" Nobody mentions the quiet desperation of those who have survived—the quiet desperation to feel human, to connect with others, to be anonymous once more.

When the woman who has been assaulted finally takes her own life after existing in misery, in agonizing desolation for nearly five months, we don't praise her. We don't refer to her now as the divine being we once called her. We certainly don't think of her as "brave." Instead, we say things like: "What a pity," "Not surprised," or, "She's in a better place now."

There's nothing glorious or wonderful about being a survivor. Those that like to hurt other people know this for a fact. Perhaps that's why they go out of their way to cause heartache, despair. Maybe they get their kicks out of knowing that someone will survive their desecration and will be forever marked by what they've done—permanently stained.

I've learned that if you want someone to truly suffer, let them live.

I sit in my car while it idles in the grocery store parking lot.

I lean over the passenger seat, opening a plastic bag filled with the various parts to build a small model airplane made from balsa wood.

A woman's voice speaks to me over the car radio.

"Now. Repeat after me," the voice tells me. "I am a kind, compassionate, and caring person."

I begin snapping the paper-thin wooden pieces in half until they're a fine assortment of needle-thin slivers.

"I am a kind, compassionate, and caring person," I say.

"People like me," the woman says.

I can't help but laugh at myself. The muscles in my throat flex as I swallow hard. The words—too difficult for me to repeat.

"People like…"

But I cannot finish the sentence.

"People are drawn to me because I am worthy of the same kindness and compassion," the woman's voice tells me.

I sense my cheeks heating red. "People are drawn to me because I am worthy of the same kindness and compassion."

I hold one of the wooden needles I've fashioned from the model airplane set and I guide the tip beneath a pinch of skin along my wrist.

"Very good," the woman says as I stab myself. "Of course, these things can be very difficult to remember when we're faced with the anxiety of meeting and connecting with other people. In social settings, be mindful to remain 'present.'

Be in your body. You have the magnificent power to draw people in and have them connect with you. Only you have that ability."

I pick up another shaving of balsa wood and I inspect my hand for my next penance.

"Look in the mirror and practice meeting a new person and connecting with them," the woman directs.

I decide on my open palm. I stab myself there.

"Remember the three important steps to building a connection. Eye contact. Firm handshake. Name. Repeat after me: Hi. My name is (blank)."

I press the splinter along the surface of my hand until it's buried beneath the skin. My eyes water at the pain.

"Hi," I say. "My name is Jillian."

"It's very nice to meet you," the woman on the recording says.

"It's very nice to meet you."

"Very good," she says. "Now. Repeat it again. Only this time, at the end, say a little something about yourself."

I lower the mirror above the steering wheel. At first, I'm hesitant to face my likeness. After much resistance, my reflection meets my gaze.

I see all color drain from my face.

"Hi," I say. "My name is Jillian. And I'm terrified of you."

———

"That's nice," the pockmarked Assistant Store Manager tells me as soon as I've introduced myself. "This way."

He clears his throat, adjusting the square-shaped eyeglasses balancing on the tip of his pimple-dotted nose.

I'm a deer in headlights.

I carry a leather almond-colored briefcase with a golden lock. There is a lanyard around my neck displaying my name, photograph, and certifications. My head is wrapped in a hair net.

I hold up the ID badge for him to approve.

The neon-colored Band-Aid glued to my wrist startles me—a gruesome reminder of my transgressions. I sense my face paling, fearful he might make some senseless comment.

He doesn't even pay it a second glance.

I lurch forward, following the Assistant Store Manager's spiritless stride through the entryway and further into the market.

"I—didn't get your name," I say to him.

I'm unsteady as I walk. My feet seem to be apprehensive in my new, expensive pair of high heels. Why had I decided to wear them today? After all, who am I trying to impress?

"11410," the Assistant Store Manager barks at me.

I look at him with the utmost concern. "Those are numbers?"

He doesn't look at me when he speaks. "They sent Isaac Newton this time."

The Assistant Store Manager ushers me into the produce section. I fumble to open my briefcase, unfolding a small notebook and loosening a pen to write.

"I'll need your name for my report," I tell him.

"No names here," he tells me. "Just numbers. Aisle twelve. Cleaners. Ziploc. Dish soap. Paper goods. Aisle eleven.

Popcorn. Candy. Chips. Aisle ten. Cereal. Crackers. What other numbers do you want?"

My eyes dart about like a trapped animal as he leads me about the maze of bins arranged with fresh fruits and vegetables.

"I was just asking—"

"Number of pounds of vegetables delivered daily. Two-hundred-seventy-five. Number of shopping carts to be accounted for at open and close. One-hundred-fifteen. Number of days until one of these idiots finds the pound of Gruyere I hid in the heat vent. To be determined."

I stammer, my breath becoming rapid, as I steer through aisles filled with customers, screaming children, and half-filled shopping carts.

"I'm afraid—I'm going to have to put that in my report," I tell him.

He looks nonplussed. "Feel free to add how Stanley in the meat department refuses to wash his hands after bathroom breaks. I don't give a rat's turd that he's been here for eleven years. The man's been diagnosed with genital warts five times. I'd stay away from the veal if I were you."

My stomach begins to curl. I feel queasy, my knees threatening to buckle.

"Is there—a bathroom?" I ask him.

The Assistant Store Manager glances at his wristwatch. "In the back. Knock first. Carlos from produce and Angela from customer service usually have it reserved at this time."

I shake my head in disbelief and attempt to center myself. "This may take me a few hours."

"Stay as long as you like," he tells me. "If you need anything, please hesitate to ask."

He throws me a look of disgust and then storms off.

The latch on my briefcase immediately responds, loosening and scattering my papers all over the tiled floor.

Employees skirt around me, whispering to one another, as I kneel to collect the mess like an invisible servant.

———

I stand behind the counter of the delicatessen, intently inspecting a thermometer inside the end of a freshly cooked chicken in a plastic container.

Once I draw the bulb out, I hold the stem under a lamp and squint to read. I shake my head at the reading and then solemnly make a note in my notebook, as if I were recording the death of a child.

Just then, I hear snickering.

The shrillness of the laughter grows louder and louder as if it were intended to attract my attention.

I lift my head and see two female employees hovering across the aisle, maliciously glancing at me and then passing soundless words between one another.

I can feel my face softening, my eyes returning to the thermometer and my notes.

I pretend not to be bothered.

Of course, I can't help but punish myself with one more look at them.

It's as if I had never grown up.

I'm lying naked on my stomach in bed. I've wrapped bedsheets around my waist as if they were Grecian robes.

Hovering over me with a paintbrush and an angelic smile is my lover, Pia. She's naked, too, her alabaster skin glowing hot in the dim candlelight.

Pia leans over me. My flesh—her canvas.

I watch her as she guides the tip of the paintbrush about my shoulder, delicately printing each letter of a short poem she has written.

She's also embroidered small, colored flowers about the verse of cursive lettering.

Music plays softly throughout my apartment.

"People stare at me because they think I'm a monster," I tell her. "And they're right. I am one."

"You're not," Pia says.

I roll my eyes at her. "That's not what you're supposed to say."

"What's that?"

I stir beneath the sheets, gentle.

"You're supposed to tell me, 'Yes. You are a monster. You're *my* monster.'"

"Hold still," Pia says, drawing the corner of a letter along my shoulder.

"Why don't you ever say that to me?" I ask her.

"Because—I'd be lying," she says.

"That I'm a monster? Or that I'm yours?"

Pia looks as though she doesn't want to answer. She does anyway.

"Both."

"I could be," I tell her. "If you wanted."

"Just because two strangers share the same bad habits, doesn't mean they belong to each other," Pia tells me.

"But we're not strangers," I say to her.

Pia doesn't look convinced.

"We are when we're dressed," she says. "Didn't you want it that way?"

For the past forty-five minutes I've been careful enough to keep my hand hidden from Pia. When I stir again, the neon-colored Band-Aid wrapped around my wrist flashes at Pia like a warning light.

"More of these—?" she asks me.

I try to disguise embarrassment with laughter.

"You're starting a collection," she says.

I sense my lips tighten. I'm quiet for a moment.

"I don't feel like a monster when I'm with you," I tell her, giggling at the obscenity of the thought. "I feel like a—swan."

Pia looks as though she were desperate to change the subject, her eyes avoiding me at all costs. Her labor has become more vigorous, earnest for any kind of distraction.

"Why a swan?" she asks.

"Because," I tell her, "that's what my dad always calls me."

"You see him much?"

Pia's question feels like a heated iron stirring in my gut. I wince a little.

"He sends a letter once a month. Tells me how much he loves me. How proud he is."

"He lives far?"

"Two-hour drive," I explain.

"And you still don't think to see him?" she asks me.

I close my eyes, wishing I were far away. "I—can't."

"Don't want to?"

"My mother—doesn't want me there," I tell her. "She said if she ever saw me again, she'd kill me."

Pia's paintwork comes to a halt.

She tucks some of my hair behind my ear with a tenderness that perplexes me for a moment.

"Jay," she says.

"I can't pretend to be angry with her. They've given me everything I could've wished for. First-class education. An apartment without rent. A brand-new car every two years. Just as long as I keep away from them."

Pia squints at me, obviously trying to comprehend. "Why?"

I take a hit from the joint on the ashtray beside the bed.

"She doesn't want me there."

"She didn't like having a daughter that liked girls?"

"She still doesn't know, probably. She sent me away to boarding school when I was nine."

"You haven't seen her since then?" Pia asks.

But I don't answer.

"Not even for holidays? Christmas?"

I close my eyes, shaking my head as she exhales a wreath of smoke.

"You're her child," Pia says.

I can sense tears webbing in the corners of my eyes.

"She told me that she never wanted me," I say. "She said I'm a monster."

I hide my face from Pia in a pillow, my soft sobs becoming muffled.

Just then, Pia pecks my neck with a kiss.

I turn to look at her, surprised by her sudden tenderness.

"You are," Pia says. "The most beautiful monster I've ever seen."

I can feel my face warming with joy. I'm startled and then suddenly anxious for another. I purse my lips for Pia's mouth, but Pia pulls away.

"You'll ruin the paint," Pia says.

"Have you finished?" I ask.

My eyes beg Pia to reach for the hand mirror on the nightstand.

Pia holds the mirror in front of me and angles it so that I can see the lettering she's printed along my shoulder.

"Read it to me?" I ask.

Pia's breath is gentle on the nape of my neck. Her fingers follow every letter she's printed with agonizing care.

"Little stars hang in an ocean where you and I will never dream. I wonder if they smell like cinnamon or lilies floating on a stream. I watch them bloom in fiery showers, smeared and dripping there like morning dew. I'll never know what they smell like, my love, but I can only imagine they smell as sweet as you."

I can scarcely speak, delirium paralyzing me.

"For—me?" I ask her.

"Who else?"

I smile at her. "It's—perfect."

"I haven't finished writing it yet," she tells me.

"I'll never want to wash it off."

Pia falls into the bed beside me. She lights a cigarette.

"Don't be stupid," she says.

"I promise."

Pia sits in the uncomfortable silence for a moment. She takes a drag.

"I didn't write it—"

Suddenly, I'm worried. "For me?"

"For you to keep forever," she says. "Nothing lasts that long."

"It's something I love," I tell her. "Everything I love, I keep."

Pia's breath whistles as she opens her mouth to speak. There's a sentence heavy on her tongue.

"Jay—"

Just then, my cellphone begins to chirp.

I stir beneath the sheets, reaching for the nightstand.

"I'll turn it off."

"No. Go ahead."

I glance at the screen and notice a number I do not recognize. I slide my thumb across the display and hold the phone to my ear.

"Hello—?"

A brittle-thin voice greets me on the other end of the line.

"Is this Jillian Finch?" the voice asks.

"Yes."

"This is Ambrose Thorn. Your mother's nurse. I'm afraid I'm the bearer of unfortunate news."

I straighten. I can sense my face flushing with dread, my heart pounding in my chest like a hammer against the head of a nail. It's not that I was expecting this call. However, I'd be lying if I didn't say that I have considered this moment again and again.

"What happened—?" I ask him.

"It's your father," Ambrose says. "I'm afraid he's passed."

The words do not register at first. Everything around me starts to blur.

"It was all very sudden," Ambrose tells me. "We've already begun making arrangements for the funeral. It'll be held next week. Your mother has requested your presence. She's wondering if you're able to come?"

I swallow hard, my esophagus burning. It feels as though someone has emptied a canister of gasoline down my throat.

"Yes," I say to him. "I'll come. Thank you for letting me know."

I end the call and stare at the wall for a moment. Out of my peripheral vision, I can see Pia glaring at me and wondering what's happened.

"Jay—?"

More tears bead in the corners of my eyes.

"My dad died," I tell her.

Pia lifts her head. "Jay."

"That was my mother's nurse," I explain. "They're making arrangements for the funeral next week."

"Jay, I'm so sorry," Pia says, her eyes lowering.

For a moment, I'm quiet. My mouth opens with muted words. Then I regard Pia.

"Turn the light off," I tell her.

"What for?" she asks me.

I'm already ripping off some of the bedsheets and touching myself. "We can go again. I want to."

But Pia throws the sheets off her. She's stamping out her cigarette and on her feet at once.

"I—can't," she says.

My eyes search her for a semblance of an explanation. "Why not?"

Pia's already searching for her clothes, hoisting the jeans about her waist and fastening her bra.

"I just can't, Jay," she tells me.

"You said you would stay the night last time," I remind her. "You promised."

Pia shakes her head at me. "Please don't hate me for doing this."

I'm on my feet now, too. I try hiding Pia's shoes from her. But Pia's growing visibly impatient, and she snatches the shoes from behind my back.

"Have a bump," I say to her. "We'll smoke and open another bottle of wine. It'll be fun. I promise."

"I just have to go," Pia tells me. "Please don't ask me again. Don't make this harder for me than it already is."

Silence falls over the small room and threatens to undo the invisible tether that had fastened us for most of the evening. I can already see the wire beginning to fray.

"P. I need you," I say to her.

But Pia is already at the bedroom door, her shoes in hand.

"Please don't say that to me."

I can sense my eyes opening and closing mechanically. A scream bottles in my throat. It's a mere whisper at first.

"You—promised."

Pia cannot and will not apologize again. She turns the door handle. She watches me for a moment, a muted word of regret hanging there in her open mouth. Then she opens the apartment door and slips out, disappearing from my sight.

Once more, I'm alone. Abandoned.

The dim candles that surround the bed begin to flicker, as if commanding the walls to shrink in on me.

I swipe an empty glass from the floor and hurl it at the wall. I scream until I'm hoarse.

"You fucking promised," I shout as the glass explodes, shattering.

My whole body seems to slump as if I were a mere doll and my puppeteer had loosened the strings.

I rise from the bed and shuffle into the bathroom, my hand cradling my stomach and its invisible wound.

I stand in the open doorway for a moment, regarding my reflection in the mirror.

After a long silence, I kneel beside the bathtub, and I turn on the shower faucet. I run the water until it hisses, scalding hot.

Then I duck beneath the shower, hands furiously scrubbing the painted lettering and embroidery along my shoulder. The oils leak like exit wounds—the dark shadow of a hand stretching itself across my body.

My sweet little Jay bird. There's no excuse for the lateness of this letter. I hope you'll forgive me.

As always, your mother and I think of you every day. We hope you think of us, too.

It's rained every day here for the past week. Your mother hopes it will help her new perennials to grow.

They didn't flourish much last year. Instead, they became food for the deer. I'll attach a picture to the letter the next time I write.

I thought of you earlier today when your mother's nurse returned from town with fresh pomegranates. I ate one and it reminded me of your favorite drink when you were a little girl— seltzer water with grenadine. It was such a happy memory.

I've sent a check to your very kind landlord to cover your rent for the next three months. I hope you're still happy there.

If you're ever able, please take a picture and send it to me. I'd love to see how you've decorated your room. I can only imagine—azaleas on the windowsill and broken seashells on the nightstand.

I wish I could write more, but your mother is already upset with me as I've neglected planting her rhododendrons for three days now. I promise I will write more next time.

Until then, be well, my beautiful little swan. All my love. Always. Dad.

I'm nine years old. I sit arranged in an upholstered leather armchair as if I were an expensive figurine.

I wear a glittering pink dress with matching ballet shoes. A satin sash with the words "Birthday Girl" written in giant letters belts my torso. A tiara sparkles on my head.

My father stands at the bureau. He's slender. Dark haired. Well-groomed and immaculately dressed. He looks at me through the mirror, hands fumbling to loosen the tie about his throat.

He eyes the half-empty glass filled with sparkling water and crimson-colored syrup I've been holding in my hand. Gently wetting his thin lips, he croons a gentle murmur.

"You're not thirsty anymore?" he asks me.

Reminded, I press my mouth against the glass, and I take a drink. My father watches the muscles in my throat move as I swallow.

"Did you enjoy your birthday?" he asks.

"Yes," I tell him.

I watch him as he unfastens his tie from his collar and begins to unbutton his dress shirt.

"And your gift?" he asks me.

My fingers tighten about the jeweled music box in my hand, admiring it. The Fabergé-egg-shaped box—gold with a sapphire trim and embellished with small gemstones.

When I wind the crank, a waltz plays and the lid lifts to reveal a mirror overlooking a miniature white swan circling about the box's stage painted to resemble the glassy surface of a lake.

"It's pretty," I tell him.

"What did you wish for?" he asks.

I cross my arms. "It won't come true."

"You think I would ever tell?" he asks.

I glance around the room, as if to make certain no one is listening. "A pet snake."

My father laughs. "Not with your mother around."

"But I would finally have a friend."

I notice my father's face pale, his lips pulling downward. He recovers quickly.

"A snake wouldn't make a very good friend," he tells me. "Especially to a sweet little Jay bird like you."

"Why do you always call me a bird? Do you think I look like one?"

I watch as my father shrugs out of his dress shirt.

"Because we're a family of swans," he explains.

"Why?" I ask him, my eyes remaining fixed on the rotating miniature swan in the center of the music box.

"Why? Well, because they stay together forever... even when they drift apart. They always return to each other... That's how we are, isn't it?"

My eyes begin to lower, my voice a mere whisper.

"Not Mommy," I say.

My father's lips tighten a little and I notice his face hardening.

"No," he says. "Maybe not Mommy... but you and me. We'll always be together... I promise."

I notice my father's hands disappear below his waist as if he were to adjust his belt. He rakes his head back and closes his eyes, exhaling.

"I feel like a swan," he says. "Don't you?"

I smile, far off and dreaming.

"I feel like a swan," I answer him.

I crank the music box again and it plays gently.

My father returns me with a smile, his unseen hands still moving below his waist.

His lips gently part, another word to be flicked from the fork of his tongue.

But the sound of his voice dims until muted as his reflection in the mirror begins to ripple like the surface of a lake.

A diamond-headed snake curls about his neck, rearing its head and violently hissing at me.

Suddenly, a single shard of glass flies out from the mirror like a jeweled hornet.

I watch in silence as my father's reflection unfurls in a glorious spiderweb.

More pellets of glass follow, flying, as the mirror explodes in the blur of a sparkling hailstorm.

I cover my eyes, mouth open in a soundless scream.

OCTOBER 16, 2021

The car windshield cracks.

A spiderweb of glass unfurls before me.

I scream, covering my eyes.

Steadying my frantic breath, I pull the keys from the ignition, and I open the door.

I climb out and skirt around the front of the vehicle.

I cover my mouth, making a noise of disgust, when I come upon the apron of my car's hood.

Lying there beside a broken tree branch is a half-dead baby sparrow choked in the embrace of a large snake.

I watch in silence as the snake tightens about its helpless prey.

Dragging the branch from the windshield, I elbow it beneath the snake and its dying victim.

The snake rears its head at me, as if charmed, and hisses fiercely.

I elbow it once more and the livid coil of scales drips off the car's hood, the gagged bird now lifeless in its suffocating cradle.

Their embrace ends in a devouring kiss as the snake stretches its jaws until the small bird's head fits inside its gaping mouth.

I return to my car, opening the passenger door and dragging my suitcase off the seat.

I turn and look up at the house I haven't seen in nearly twenty years—a French Provincial-styled manor.

The steep, high roof. The imperial-looking doorways set in arched openings. The dramatic double French windows decorated with shutters.

The giant house seems to look down upon me as if I were a mere insect.

Suitcase in hand, I move up the front steps and reach the arched doorway.

I stiffen as I begin to set down my bag—the very last opportunity to turn around and leave.

I think of it for a moment.

Without another opportunity for hesitation, I press the button and the doorbell chimes sweetly.

It's not long before the door creaks open and a gaunt-looking face greets me.

The person standing there is a well-manicured specimen of a gentleman.

Although the lines about his easily frowning mouth and dark circles beneath his eyes confess his age, his trim body is outfitted with enough embellishments to retain a semblance of youth.

Dressed impeccably in all black and groomed as meticulously as possible, he speaks with an affection that resurrects the classic Hollywood glamor of cinema's finest leading men.

He tips his glasses, quizzically studying me.

"Yes?" he says.

"I'm Jillian," I say, swallowing hard. "I spoke with Ambrose—"

"You spoke with me on the phone," he says.

I exhale, letting my guard down for a moment.

"Nice to meet you."

Like a child remembering politeness, I hold out my hand. Ambrose shakes it coldly and returns me a sour look.

"My windshield—"

"You're shorter in person," he says.

I find myself stammering, unsure what to say.

"I'm—sorry?"

Then Ambrose eyes my luggage.

"Do you need help with your bags?" he asks, rolling his eyes at me.

"No," I tell him. "Just this one."

"Good."

Ambrose saunters back into the foyer, leaving me there.

After I turn to close the door, I creep inside—the impossibly large entryway threatening to grow even larger and swallow me whole. It seems so peculiar to me—how the house has not diminished in size, but rather seems so much more colossal than I had remembered. Usually, childhood homes shrink in size when you return to them. At least that's what I've been told. But not this place. For some inexplicable reason, the house seemed to become even bigger in my absence, like some cruel magic trick at my expense.

I move mechanically, gliding past the small dust-covered table arranged with a vase of dead pansies. I can't help but notice my body has become dramatically stiff, as if it knows for certain that I do not belong here.

Perhaps it's true.

It does not feel like home.

I see the moth-eaten velvet drapes robing each of the entryway's windows. All the shutters are closed, little flickers of light peeking through the slits.

My eyes scan the walls—the paper peeling in thick bunches, smashed light fixtures without light bulbs, empty picture frames.

I'm so distracted that I trample into the table arranged in the center of the hallway.

My hands tremble to grab the vase, but it's too late.

It flies off the table and shatters on the floor, little pieces skating in every direction.

Cheeks reddening, I bend down to pick up the mess. I look up and notice Ambrose waiting for me at the banister.

"I've been meaning to throw those away," he says, so matter-of-factly.

"I—I'm so sorry," I say. "I—don't know why I did that."

"You don't care for pansies?" he asks. "Me neither. They make me think of elementary school."

I glare at him, uncertain. "Why's that?"

He throws me a look that tells me I should have immediately known. "Don't play stupid."

I kneel again, gathering the shattered remains of the vase and piling the broken bits on the small table.

"I'll clean it up for you," I tell him.

"And keep your mother waiting even longer? She expected you sooner than this."

"When did it happen?" I ask him.

"Last Sunday evening," he tells me. "I found him in the morning."

I swallow nervously, hesitant to even ask. "Where is—?"

"Being prepared now," Ambrose says. "All the arrangements have already been made."

I can sense more tears threatening in the corners of my eyes, but I'll be damned if I'm going to break down and sob in front of a complete stranger.

"Why am I here then?" I ask him.

"I told you on the phone," Ambrose says. "She asked for you. Begged, actually."

"Where is she?" I ask.

"Upstairs. She wasn't sure if you'd come."

He leads me to the staircase. Just then, Ambrose turns and inspects me. I recoil almost immediately.

"What is it—?"

"You don't look anything like the pictures," he says. "You must be worried that she won't recognize you."

Ambrose starts up the staircase. I follow close behind.

"Why wouldn't she?" I ask, my voice a sullen whisper, hardly disguising my hurt. "It's only been twenty years."

As I inch further up the stairs, my eyes are immediately drawn to the jeweled chandelier hanging above the foyer.

Suddenly, I notice something I had not remembered. Or, perhaps I once had, but had forgotten until now.

Something hidden. Something truly monstrous.

A small golden sculpture of a fanged serpent hidden behind the hanging gems and coiled about the chandelier's neck.

There is the faintest whisper of a dim, rattling sound.

———

Ambrose opens the large Sapele mahogany-paneled doorway leading to my mother's bedroom. It creaks, as if it were admonishing me.

My breath whistles as I step further in, Ambrose behind her.

"I'll leave you to your reunion," he says. "Scream if you need anything. I'll be back to haunt you."

Ambrose leaves.

I turn, inching further into the room, and my mouth hangs open at the horrible sight.

My mother—a lavishly mummified body surrounded by a deafening symphony of machines that keep her preserved.

Her crown of gray hair is secreted by a pleated blue turban embroidered with gemstones.

A sleek-looking electronic apparatus belts her throat. A white cloth is also scarfed about her neck like a clerical collar.

Her nostrils are plugged with wires fed by an oxygen tank that chirps beside her enormous throne-like bed.

The machines surrounding her pulse a dim hum like a hive of honeybees. Her body occasionally shudders, releasing obscene-sounding vibrations.

Then, the wrinkled face I thought I would never see again turns, and looks directly at me with a hideously baleful look.

I soar out of the room, slamming the door shut behind me.

The blaring concerto of my mother's suffering is silenced for now.

I pant violently, curling myself into a ball and tucking into a corner of the hallway. It isn't long before Ambrose locates me there, his eyes dimmed and glassy looking. I squint at him with a wordless question at first, but he doesn't respond.

"Why didn't—you tell me?" I finally ask him.

"What was I supposed to say?"

I cover my mouth, unsure. "What—happened to her?"

"Is she not well?" Ambrose asks, concerned.

"She's a corpse," I shout at him.

"Your father tried to see that she was taken care of."

"What happened?"

"He never told you?"

I merely look at him, mouth open without understanding.

"I'm sure he told you they had hired a caretaker for her."

"Yes. But I never thought—"

"Don't let the Dowager Empress fool you," Ambrose tells me. "She's doing much better these days."

I shudder at the horrible thought of my mother languishing there while machines keep her alive.

"She doesn't look—better."

"Her voice is getting stronger, too," Ambrose explains. "Of course, they say it will never heal completely."

"Why?"

"The doctors aren't optimistic."

"No. Why wouldn't her voice be stronger?"

Ambrose smiles. "You'll be glad to know she's made such progress in the last twenty years."

"Twenty?"

"Yes?"

"From what?"

Ambrose looks at me, bewildered.

"Your father never told you?" he asks again.

I can't respond. My eyes merely beg him for an answer I'm already dreading.

"About the accident?" he asks.

"What accident?"

"When your mother tried to kill herself."

The words are like small daggers inside me. I turn away from him, my eyes closing.

"I'm sorry," he says gently. "I thought you knew. I assumed your father told you."

"What happened?" I ask.

Ambrose shakes his head. "He kept it from you for a reason."

"A letter a month for twenty years. The pages might as well have been blank."

Ambrose gestures further up the hallway, that I might follow him.

"Maybe you'd prefer to see your room now?" he asks.

But my hand soon becomes a tourniquet on Ambrose's arm, squeezing tight.

"Tell me. Please," I beg him.

"I only know what your father told me," he says.

It hurts me to finally admit it.

"You knew him better than I did."

———

Ambrose guides me through the garden.

Wind gently lifts the overgrown curtain of vines hanging along the brick wall that surrounds the small park.

Hints of a once meticulously manicured garden are now washed out entirely by a decaying jungle of weeds and climbing plants.

The tableau of monstrous greenery beckons a visual of prehistoric times when lizard-like beasts roamed about enormous forests of ferns.

"The doctors say that the damage done to her spinal cord is irreversible," Ambrose explains to me. "At one time, your father was hopeful she might. But they've insisted she'll never walk again."

"She—hasn't left her bed in twenty years?"

But Ambrose will not answer.

"How could he not tell me?"

"Her vocal cords were injured in the fall as well," Ambrose tells. "Like I said, they've improved quite a bit. She still needs a special device in order to speak."

I fold my arms, closing my eyes. "I should never have come back here."

"You don't mean that."

"This isn't home," I tell him, shaking my head.

"Was it ever?"

"I don't think home exists when you grow up," I say. "It's something you lose and forget about. Like an old pair of shoes or baby teeth. Home is—something you outgrow."

"She told me she needed you," Ambrose says.

"You think I care?"

"You look like you do."

I turn away from him.

I begin to watch a small black velvet-bodied spider sew a web along the rim of an empty, sun-bleached birdbath.

"When I was little, I used to write my diary in the third person because I saw an old black-and-white movie with Elizabeth Taylor and that's what she did," I say. "I would write things like, 'She saw a robin today.' Or, 'She was so happy today because father bought her a new pair of patent-leather shoes.' I would tear the pages out and hide them all over the house. I used to play a game and count the days until either my mother or my father found them. One day, I tore a page out that I had written only six words on. 'She wished her mother loved her.' I hid it beneath her pillow. But, when I went to look for it the next day, I found it had been crumpled up and thrown away. Why should I care about her when she treats a piece of paper better than me?"

I rise from the bench and start to move toward the archway that leads out of the garden.

Ambrose hastens after me.

"I've been lying to you," he says.

I turn slightly. "What's that?"

"About your mother," he says. "Her doctor is not as optimistic on her progress as I've made it sound. She stays here because she can afford to. Not because of her health. In fact, he seems to think she hasn't very much time left at all."

"How long?" I ask him.

"A month," he tells me. "Maybe less."

"Then I guess you'll call me in another month?"

Ambrose hesitates slightly. "You're not going to see her?"

I pause, carefully considering each and every word.

"I'll stay until the funeral. Hopefully by then someone can fix my car."

"She tells me she's scared," Ambrose says.

I laugh, genuinely amused at the thought of my wretched mother being frightened.

"Of what?"

"She won't say," Ambrose tells me. "Something in the house. She's begged me every night to stay until you came."

If my tongue could, I'd flick out beads of venom.

"What's another month after twenty years?"

"She may not be here then," Ambrose says.

"As long as that's a promise she can keep."

I glide under the archway, down the stone steps, and out onto the lawn. Ambrose trails me close behind.

I nearly slip on the final step as I lift my head. It's then that I see something so bewildering, so perplexing that it paralyzes me completely. My mouth hangs open, as if desperately trying to comprehend.

A giant pyramid of junked antique furniture.

Perhaps the most expensive pile of rubbish in the world.

Eighty feet high and wide, the impossibly colossal monument looks just like a sleeping beast with a barbed spine.

A menagerie of wasted opulence. Desks made of French walnut. Empty bookcases and dressers fashioned from English elm. Doors engraved with ornate illustrations and built from the finest West Indian mahogany.

All heaped together as if they were sticks of kindling for a giant's bonfire.

I circle the monstrosity, uncertain.

Ambrose is at my shoulder like a devilish imp.

"I was waiting for you to see it," he tells me.

My eyes never leave the pyramid, an invisible lasso about my throat drags me closer toward it.

"What—is it?"

"Your father's collection," Ambrose says. "The man had the finest taste in antiques."

"Who did this?" I ask, my eyes still searching the menagerie for an explanation.

"Your mother ordered it to be done the day after he passed."

I glance at Ambrose. "Why?"

"I tried to arrange movers to clear everything into storage. But she was adamant that it all be removed from the house and junked immediately."

Without warning, a thought arrives in the center of my mind.

"Did you find—a music box?" I ask him.

"A music box?"

"In the shape of a golden egg and decorated with gemstones. There was a mirror and a revolving miniature white swan inside."

Ambrose's eyes lower. "I'm sorry. I imagine it ended up in there."

I creep closer toward the mountain of antique furniture. I reach out, cautious to touch a bureau's leg of white oak. If only I could blaze right through the pile to find my lost souvenir. I think of doing it, but Ambrose's voice stops me at once.

"I wouldn't get too close if I were you," he says.

"Why not?"

"In only a week's time, all types of wildlife have been curious," Ambrose explains. "Birds and squirrels. But snakes especially. It's their home now."

The wind hisses, murmuring like distant voices all around me.

———

With my back pressed against the wall, I'm sitting in the corner of my mother's bedroom. I watch her as she sleeps, the collection of machines surrounding her whispering to me that I'm not welcome here, that I should leave at once.

I fold my arms and catch sight of myself in the armoire's mirror. It looks as if I'm merely waiting for my mother to die.

I let my face soften and uncross my arms until they're hanging at my sides.

My mother stirs gently, eyes opening. She sees me immediately and a delicate breath escapes her.

I'm quiet, however.

I wince when my mother speaks, the electronic device belting her throat flashing a white light at me. It obviously pains her to talk—her every breath a labor, her every word rehearsed.

Her brittle-thin voice is disguised with an electronic hiss, and it screeches at me, bug-like.

"My little Jay bird," she says to me. "I knew you'd come."

I stare at my mother. What could I possibly say?

"I waited so long," she says.

More silence fills the room.

"I'm glad you did. Come sit by me—?"

I turn away from my mother, gazing out the dust-covered window.

"So you can keep your promise?" I ask her.

My mother's wrinkled lips pucker slightly, her eyes searching me for a semblance of an explanation.

"You forgot?" I ask her.

I glance in the mirror and notice my stare of hatred has returned and stretched itself across my face. I hold out my neck for my mother as if it were an invitation.

"That you'd kill me if you ever saw me again," I whisper.

My mother's face thaws a little.

"Jay bird," she says. "Please come here."

My resolve begins to weaken for some inexplicable reason, as if my mother has somehow undone some of my determination. She was capable of such things, and I knew this to be true.

I notice my mother begin to search my face. The old woman is choked for a moment, as if some invisible wraith has seized her tongue.

"You look—beautiful," she says. "My little swan."

My eyes lower. I bite my lip until it turns purple, and I can taste a bit of blood.

"Now that he's gone you can be free," she tells me.

I can hardly believe what she's saying. "Now that —he's—gone?"

"I waited for this day," she tells me. "I always imagined how it would be."

"How the fuck can you say that? He loved me."

My mother's voice firms. "He never loved anything. He was a monster."

"Just like me?" I ask her.

"Jillian—"

"Is that why you've thrown out everything he ever collected?" I ask.

My mother shakes her head gently, as if attempting to hurl the very thought of my beloved father from her mind. "I wanted every bit of him out of this house. I'm going to order Ambrose to buy a few gallons of gasoline and a matchbook."

I turn away, covering my mouth. "I knew this was a mistake."

"You can come home now," she whispers to me.

"This was never my home."

"It can be," my mother says. "I want it to be. I want you—I need you to stay."

I whimper a little. A pathetic laugh.

"You need me?"

My mother sighs. "Jay bird. I can't tell you how much it's pained me to keep you away all these years."

"You don't need me," I bark at her. "You don't need anybody. You never have."

My mother's polite pleading turns to panicked desperation.

"I'm scared," she says, her eyes widening. "I need you to stay here with me."

"Scared of what?" I ask her.

My mother's trembling voice softens to a dread-filled whisper.

"I think there's... *something* inside the house," she tells me. "I hear it at night."

My mother grabs hold of my hand. Her fingers tighten

about mine and squeeze so fiercely that I wonder if she'll snap my hand from my wrist.

"I don't want to be here alone," she tells me. "Please. Promise that you'll stay."

I finally drag my hand out of my mother's steely grasp.

"I'll stay until the funeral," I tell her.

Of course, it's not exactly what I would prefer, but I can't go anywhere until my windshield is fixed.

My mother heaves a little, her insect-like voice ringing.

"Jillian Rose," she says.

Perhaps once I might have trembled with fear. I might have lowered my head with shame or covered my face to hide reddened cheeks. But I'm strong and without any pity now.

"You could say no to your mother?" she asks me.

I stare blankly at her.

"You were never a mother," I say to her. "You never will be."

MAY 16, 2001

I'm nine years old, still dressed in my favorite pink party gown.

I skirt along the corridor, gripping a small wooden model airplane in my hands as if it were a precious animal.

I come upon the large door leading to my parents' bedroom.

A sliver of light collects on the floor of the hallway, their silhouettes flickering in the dim glow.

I crouch, listening as they quarrel.

"Out," my mother says. "I want her gone by tomorrow."

"Lorelai. Please be reasonable."

Just then, I hear glass shattering as if something were tossed against a wall.

"Don't you fucking touch me," my mother shrieks at him. "I want her as far away from here as possible. I never want to see her again."

I squat beside the door, clearing some of the wetness from both of my eyes as I keep my ear pinned against the wall.

"I'm not waiting another week," my mother tells him. "I want her gone tomorrow morning."

My father seems to hesitate, stammering with unsureness. "You know I could never—"

"Yes. Say it."

The dreadful silence nearly paralyzes me as I wait for my father to answer her.

Finally, he does.

"Yes," he says. "Tomorrow."

"I'll do it myself," my mother tells him.

I hear footsteps nearing the open doorway. I duck out of the light and into a nearby alcove, holding my breath.

"I can't say goodbye to her?" my father asks.

"What would you need to say goodbye to her for?"

I realize only too late that I've been squeezing the model airplane in my hands, clutching tighter and tighter every time I listen to my mother speak. Just then, the model snaps in half and a splinter stabs my open palm.

I cry out and, for a moment, I'm worried they might have

heard me. But quite suddenly I'm careless and not concerned about them in the slightest. I'm much more preoccupied with the wondrous sensation of the sliver pinching me beneath my skin. It's almost too much for me to bear. Suddenly, it's a horrible feeling that I want to experience again and again.

After all, it's what I deserve.

OCTOBER 18, 2021

I notice a drop of my blood lands in the center of the embroidered white-linen napkin I'm holding.

My face reddens with embarrassment as I plug my leaking nose and nervously glance about the room.

I'm an island set in a sea of solemn-faced, expensively dressed guests milling about the catered reception. Some glare at me with unforgiving scowls as if I were an uninvited guest.

The sound of their chatter dims as I retreat to a corner of the dining room, napkin stuffed in my nostril.

Since the dining room table has been recently junked, the candles and silver serving platters of gourmet cuisine have been arranged on a carpet of white linen along the floor.

The guests, however, seem to think nothing of the unusual arrangement. They're far too preoccupied with their gossip.

Servers carrying trays of canapes glide past me and ignore my plea for another napkin.

An older woman, dressed in a chic black dress and matching leather pumps, is suddenly at my side.

Her Audrey Hepburn-esque pixie wig is so rich and full it could possibly masquerade as real if it weren't slightly lopsided.

While her face is sweet-looking with a youthful naivete, it's caked with so much makeup that she appears as if she were an embalmed drag queen.

"No pomegranates today?" the old woman asks me.

For a moment, I'm lost. Then, as I squint and look closer, I recognize the woman as my Aunt Trixie.

Without warning, I'm swallowed in a seemingly permanent embrace.

"Even after twenty years, you're silly enough to think I wouldn't recognize my favorite niece?" she asks me.

Aunt Trixie squeezes me tighter, and it feels as though my face were turning purple. Finally, she releases me.

"Your only niece," I say, choking.

"To hell with Dr. Miller's prescription glasses," she says, removing her dark, mirror-like glasses. "I don't care if he's the most respected optometrist in the state. His eyewear is not Balenciaga. It belongs on corpses."

Just then, she realizes her poor word choice. She glances around.

"Oh, dear. Wrong place," she says.

I watch her as she downs another gulp from her wine glass.

"Jillian Rose. You look positively divine," she says. "As charming as I remember. Do you even eat? So much like your father. Christ in a Prada swimsuit, you have his eyes."

I smile at her, awkwardly, unsure how to receive the

compliment. It feels strange to think I possess something from the man I've worshipped since I was a little girl—the man I hardly know anything about.

Aunt Trixie's tone changes, her voice lowering as if out of respect.

"I'm so sorry, dear," she says. "We all are."

Aunt Trixie hooks her arm underneath mine and begins to guide me through the dining room scattered with funeral guests.

"Do you remember when you were a little girl, you'd come to the house we would rent next door every summer and you'd beg to pick the pomegranates?"

I'm hardly relieved at the memory, but I try to at least pretend that I am. I lower my eyes as we pass more grimacing mouths whispering about me.

"They were always my favorite," I tell my aunt.

"Your father's, too," Aunt Trixie says. "You'd both walk over to our garden with your darling baskets and leave with them filled to the brim. Then you'd make something with them. What was it? Jam?"

"Grenadine," I tell her.

She simpers, visibly maudlin about the whole ordeal. "You and your father's sweet teeth."

It's then that I notice my phone screen lighting up with a call from Pia, my phone starting to vibrate. I think to answer it. But not now. I have nothing to say to her. I don't know if I'll ever have anything to say to her ever again.

I flick my thumb across the screen to ignore the call and Pia's picture vanishes from the display.

"Your uncle and I were devastated when we first heard the news," Aunt Trixie tells me. "We thought he'd outlive us all. Bless the man. The picture of health."

It dawns on me that I could perhaps ask Aunt Trixie. She might be able to tell me, after all. I pull her closer and I lower my voice until it's a soft whisper.

"Do you know—how he—?"

Aunt Trixie looks at me, perplexed. "He—?"

"Passed away—?"

Aunt Trixie's eyes search me, as if surprised. "You mean they never told you?"

I merely shake my head at her, hiding my discomfort.

"We assumed it was heart related," Aunt Trixie tells me. "They never told us. You don't know?"

I purse my lips. What words are there left to say?

Aunt Trixie pulls me tighter and slowly we make our way into the drawing room.

Guests are milling about the sun-washed room with their drinks in hand.

Much of the furniture in the room has been cleared out and junked, imprints of years' worth of wear remaining like dark shadows on the wooden floor and carpet.

My mother is seated on her throne, her assortment of machines flanking her like obedient servants. Several guests surround her and offer their muted condolences.

Aunt Trixie and I stand in the doorway, watching my mother as she receives her guests the way royalty might accept their most loyal subjects.

"Your mother looks well since the last time I saw her,"

Aunt Trixie tells me. "Shame she couldn't be with us at the cemetery."

"You see her much?" I ask.

Aunt Trixie shakes her head. "I doubt she'll say two words to me."

In my peripheral vision, I watch as Aunt Trixie empties the remainder of her wine glass and slams it down on a tray as a server passes.

"My sister was always like that," she says. "Family doesn't always mean 'same.' Or 'sane' for that matter. I certainly wouldn't have chosen pastel-colored drapes for this room."

I swallow hard. There's a question fizzing in my throat that's begging to be asked.

"Were you told when she—?"

Aunt Trixie cocks her head at me. "When she—?"

I glance away for a moment. "Tried to kill herself."

"We were vacationing in Mozambique when it happened," she tells me. "Your father wrote to us. Why?"

I nervously shove my hands into my pockets, my eyes avoiding Aunt Trixie. "No reason."

Her eyes narrow to mere slits. "They didn't tell you?"

I stammer. I can feel my cheeks heating red. "No. Of course, they—told me. I was just wondering. Do you know why?"

"Pardon?"

"Do you know why she—?"

But I can't bear to finish the question. I think of flagging down one of the handsome servers and requesting a drink, but unexpectedly there are none to be found.

"I suppose the poor woman abandoned all hope after she lost—"

Just then, Aunt Trixie's mouth snaps shut and severs the remainder of the sentence as if she were a steel trap. She pauses, her skin flushing.

"Lost what?" I ask her.

But Aunt Trixie recovers quickly.

"—the will to go on," she says. "She was dreadfully upset when you left, you know?"

"She told you that?"

"It was obvious," Aunt Trixie says. "I'm sure she's delighted you're home now."

Aunt Trixie and I watch as Ambrose delivers a glass of water to my mother. She thanks his kindness with a smile.

"That's not the only thing she's delighted with," Aunt Trixie says. "I've heard she's quite smitten with that special nurse of hers. He might look Italian, but I think he takes more after the Greeks, if you know what I mean. He's been seen with men of all ages."

I fold my arms, watching Ambrose care for my mother in a way that I know I'll never be able to.

"As long as I don't have to take care of her."

"He might be taking care of the dear woman too much. My sister, bless her. She probably doesn't suspect a thing. Poor lamb."

"What do you mean?" I ask her.

Just then, Aunt Trixie clutches my arm and pulls me into the corridor, lowering her voice. She's salivating, emphatically delivering every unsavory detail.

"I've been told he's been out and about in her car making very expensive purchases," she says. "Givenchy. Louis Vuitton. Yves Saint Laurent. Last time I checked, your mother does not wear a men's size twelve Ferragamo patent-leather loafer. The man has taste."

My eyes return to Ambrose as he stands beside my mother. His lips are at her ear, whispering, and she's grinning at him like a reverent dog.

"You think he's stealing from her?" I ask Aunt Trixie.

"She could simply be spoiling him the way a mother pampers a child," Aunt Trixie explains to me. "If I were you, I'd keep an eye on that one like bad weather. I didn't want to say it. But I'd be tickled to know if anything has been changed with the will. Both hers and your father's."

I turn away for a moment. Out of the corner of my eye, I can't help but notice Aunt Trixie eyeing me up and down the same way a starving mantis stalks a fly.

"You haven't seen it yet, have you?" she asks me.

"What?"

"The will."

I shake my head. That's the furthest thought from my mind right now.

"No. Not yet," I tell her.

But Aunt Trixie can't seem to be pleased. She's as gentle as a chainsaw when she wants something.

"Your father—said he would be kind to me," she says. "Mary Magdalene in Armani boots, the man had more money than God. I'd be devastated to learn some—*male nurse* has robbed us of what's rightfully ours."

I notice Aunt Trixie glaring at Ambrose, as if she were imagining squishing him like a pathetic mealworm. Perhaps that's exactly what he is. But that doesn't matter to me now. Nothing does.

"I don't care about that," I tell my aunt. "What I want, I'll never have again. I want my father back."

The whole room seems to slow, the dim sound of the guests surrounding me beginning to boom until their chatter is a pulse like a symphony of crickets at dusk.

———

The silence after the storm is as deafening as the guests' chatter.

I sit in the center of the sofa like a doll arranged by her owner. I stare blankly out at the empty room littered with half-filled wine glasses and half-finished plates of food.

Ambrose loiters in the doorway.

"Your mother's asleep now," he announces.

I won't look at him.

"Good," I say.

"Beautiful service," Ambrose says. "Pity you weren't able to speak on behalf of your father."

I can't tell whether Ambrose is trying to hurt me or heal me. Either way, he's most unwelcome in my presence.

"I called the repair shop for you," he tells me. "The soonest they can send a mechanic is the day after tomorrow."

Ambrose is motionless, as if waiting for a comment of gratitude, thankfulness, anything. I leave him wanting.

"You know, I'm your mother's nurse," he says. "Not yours."

Just as he's about to turn to leave, it occurs to me again that perhaps he knew my father better than anyone else. It pains me to think that a perfect stranger might have known my father better than his only child.

"Ambrose," I say.

He pivots, turning to face me.

My breath is shallow, nervousness thickening my tongue. "Can you—tell me—about him? Stories? Anything?"

I wince a little, devastated to admit that I have so few.

A look of pity floods Ambrose's face as he regards me.

"The man said two words to me every day for ten years," he says. "Not much of a story, I'm afraid."

Ambrose leaves, visibly upset to have wounded me so terribly.

The unbearable quiet surrounds me once more.

I rise from the sofa and cross to the small antique record player that's been dumped on the floor. It sits inside the stain of a square outline of what must have once been a large bureau.

I rest the needle on the disc and Schubert begins to play.

Just then, I notice a small inscription that's been carved into the wood of the record player. I read the words with my fingers: "For J. Love, Mom."

I snatch the needle from the disc and slam the lid shut.

I grab the record player and toss on my coat.

The round light of my flashlight flickers like a firefly as I hasten down the steps from the house. Wind chases me as I skirt across the grass, the record player tucked beneath my arm.

I reach the pyramid and my determination abandons me almost instantly as I gaze up at the impossible mountain of piled furniture. I might as well be a small morsel for a giant beast.

My resolve finally returning, I dump the wooden box like a thankless offering.

Just as I drop it, a long, thin rope of scales darts past my feet and disappears into the menagerie of antique wood.

I jump, quieting my breath and motionless, waiting for the horrible creature to return. After a moment, I turn and meander back toward the house.

I shut the door behind me as I enter, and set the flashlight down on the flowerless walnut credenza. I admire it for a moment, wondering why it hasn't been junked with the others.

I open a drawer and find a small note inside. I unfold the paper, already yellowing with antiquity, and read the sentence scrawled in pencil: "She visited Aunt Trixie's garden and picked pomegranates today."

It's as if I have found a long-lost child once thought dead.

My lips quiver and I rub my eyes.

I fold the paper and I stuff the note inside my pocket.

I wander into the library. What was once a precisely manicured archive is now a giant pyre of books. All the antique wooden cases have been removed and now thousands of books are scattered about the floor.

I spot a large oak bureau remaining in the corner of the room.

That's an unusual relic to keep, I think to myself.

Unfastening the handle and opening one of the engraved

doors, a deluge of sheets filled with pencil drawings I had done when I was a child pour out from the shelves. A shower of writing utensils (crayons, pencils, paintbrushes) falls out as well.

My eyes scan every sheet—drawings of the garden, bird nests, trees, flowers. I leaf through each paper, the sheets falling at my feet.

Suddenly, something catches my attention. Something tucked between one of the drawers inside the bureau.

Another note I had hidden when I was a child.

I unfold the piece of paper and read the handwriting: "She wishes she didn't have to leave her home today. She'll be leaving forever."

I think of crumpling the paper, but I stop in utter bewilderment. I notice three crayon-written words in handwriting I cannot recognize at the bottom of the note: "Please help me. Down." There is a crudely drawn arrow pointing downward beside the lettering.

I'm so mesmerized by the note that I don't notice Ambrose standing in the doorway, gazing at me, until he speaks.

"Anything else before I leave?" he asks.

I nearly leap out of my skin. He seems to immediately notice that my face has drained of all color.

"What is it?" he asks me.

"Nothing," I tell him, shoving the note into my pocket.

"My phone number is on the kitchen table," Ambrose says. "Call if you need anything. Try not to need anything until tomorrow between nine and six."

I nod, somewhat breathless. It's a few moments before I'm panting like a feral cat in heat.

"You'll be okay?" he asks.

I force a less than convincing smile. "Yes. Of course. See you tomorrow."

Ambrose rolls his eyes and slips out into the foyer and eventually disappears from my sight.

I dip my hand into my pocket and fish out the small sheet of crumpled paper. I go over the words in the writing I do not recognize again and again, urgently trying to remember, the same way I do when I regard old photographs of my father.

JULY 6, 2000

I'm sitting on a stone bench in a white dress and a matching hat.

My father is on his knees beside one of the garden hedges, his gloved hands working a pair of shears as he prunes the greenery.

The lush greens of the garden are bathed in the golden glow of summer's sun.

The petals of oleander and hydrangea draped in knots about the lawn sparkle with droplets of dew.

Birds splash in the small birdbath beside the hedge-flanked stone pathway.

I carefully read from my French textbook but can't help becoming easily distracted by the hummingbirds and butterflies that flit past my face.

"Être," my father says. "Present tense. Without looking."

I shut the textbook, closing my eyes.

"Je—"

"—suis," I say.

He nods, impressed. "Tu—"

"—es."

My father smiles at me while he prunes. "Il—"

"—est."

"Nous—"

I hesitate for a moment. "—sommes."

"Vous—"

When I'm certain he's not looking, I tip the textbook slightly and peel back the page to read. Suddenly, my father's eyes snap to me.

"Jillian Rose," he barks.

I slam the book shut, grinning coyly at him. He can't ever stay mad at me.

Just then, I glance up at the blue canopy of sky above us and notice a jetliner flying overhead, contrails as thin as threads following the plane.

"Daddy," I say. "What's that?"

My father glances up at the sky and then back at me. He crosses his arms.

"Has the sun gotten to your head, little Jay bird?" he asks. "You know what a plane looks like."

"Is it in outer space?" I ask.

"No," he says. "But close. Looks like a ghost, doesn't it?"

"It isn't, though?" I ask. "Is it?"

"No. It's not."

"Where's it going?" I ask him.

I watch my father as he smears some of the sweat from his brow, rising from his knees.

"Somewhere far away," he tells me.

My eyes lower. "I hope I never have to go there."

"Why's that?"

"I never want to leave this place."

My father pecks me on the forehead with a kiss. "This will always be your home, Jay bird."

Without warning, a rattlesnake springs out from the nearby hedge. My father leaps as the little creature begins to glide down the stone path, dragging with it a transparent hose of old skin like a bridal train.

I hasten after the snake.

"Jillian," my father calls out. "No."

The snake begins to slow over the gravel, more skin unfurling from it and stretching like a latex glove.

"Please can I keep it?" I ask my father.

"Don't get too close," he tells me.

"What's it dragging with it?" I ask.

"Old skin," he says. "It's shedding right now."

"Why?"

"To grow more," my father tells me. "To remove any parasites that may have attached to the old skin."

I crouch beside the creature as it stirs in place, more skin peeling from its tail.

"Notice how it always moves forward, Jay bird? A snake doesn't glance back and think to itself, *This skin was once mine*. A snake always moves forward. Keeps changing. No matter what."

"It hurts?" I ask my father.

"It always hurts to change," he says.

"It shouldn't. It should just stay as it was."

"It can't," my father tells me, his head lowering. "Nothing can."

"Not even me?" I ask.

My father pulls me a little tighter against him. "Except for you, little Jay bird."

Together, we watch the snake pull free from the last rope of skin. I can feel the warmth of my father's breath heating my ear.

"I'll stay the way I am?" I ask him.

My father merely nods.

"For how long?" I ask.

Just then, my father's mouth is at my ear. He's whispering words that seem to flood my mind and melt almost instantly as a gust of wind lifts my hair to hide the wickedness of our secrets.

The snake begins to rear its head at the both of us and hisses.

I'm startled by the sound, and I trip backward, crying out.

The snake darts at us again, its tail trembling violently with a final warning. But my father is already on his feet, brandishing the shears.

I watch in silence as my father cups the snake's head between both blades and snaps the bow shut.

Both ends of the snake slip from between the edges and scatter to the ground.

I rush to my father's arms.

"Stay there," he tells me.

"Why did you kill it?" I ask him.

My father uses the tip of the blade to poke both twitching ends of the dying snake—as if to torture it a little further, as if to make it rightly suffer for what it had done.

"It tried to bite me," he says. "It would've tried to hurt you, too."

"You didn't have to kill it," I tell him.

"Yes. I did," he says. "Sometimes to heal, you must hurt something."

There's a dim rattling sound all around us.

I watch as my father kneels, wrenching the very last bit of old skin from the snake's lifeless rattle.

OCTOBER 19, 2021

I watch quietly as Ambrose dumps a long, thin transparent coil of snakeskin onto a silver tray. It lands with a moist, crunching sound.

I wince a little and make a noise of disgust at the vile sight.

"Inside the house this time," he tells me, gloating the way a cat does when delivering a fresh kill to its owner.

"Where?" I ask him.

"The crawl space beneath the stairs," Ambrose says. "I find them in the garden all the time. Never in the house before."

I watch as he begins to prepare a pot of tea to bring to my mother upstairs. He alternates between heating the water and eating a hard-boiled egg.

"Where do you think they're coming from?" I ask.

"That pile of junk outside isn't enough for them, I suppose," he says with such venom. "They want to claim the whole house now, too."

I flinch at the word "junk." It feels so callous, so careless to refer to memories from my childhood as rubbish.

"It's not junk," I say to him.

Ambrose seems to understand, flashing me a soundless apology.

"I see at least two a day," he says, pouring the heated water into an empty teapot.

"You're not going to wash your hands?" I ask him.

Ambrose rolls his eyes and begins to run his hands under the water faucet with soap. Meanwhile, I take the glass dome arranged on the kitchen table beside me and cover the platter of snakeskin with it.

As Ambrose shifts gently, his neatly shined and expensive-looking patent-leather loafers crinkle.

"Those are beautiful shoes," I tell him.

Ambrose grins with all the sheepishness of a door-to-door salesman. "Your mother's idea. She hated seeing me in sneakers every day."

"They must have been—expensive."

Ambrose's face seems to flicker with guilt only for a moment. "Your mother's a very generous woman."

I fold my arms, turning away from him. "I wouldn't know."

"They must be coming in from somewhere," Ambrose says.

But I'm too distracted by the sight of a small black spider scurrying along the length of the windowsill. I think about how wondrous it must be to be a small insect—to feel no urgency to know your parents, to want only to survive.

"Jillian—?"

I turn back to Ambrose and realize I've somehow drifted off.

"Sorry," I say to him.

"You're not frightened?" he asks me.

"I wanted one when I was little," I tell him, a little apprehensive to confess something so decidedly unusual. "I used to think their diamond-shaped heads were pretty."

"Diamond-shaped anything is pretty," Ambrose says, arranging the serving tray with the teacup, sugar, and milk.

"Can't you do anything about it?" I ask Ambrose. "Call someone to have them removed? I don't want them in my house."

Ambrose swivels to me almost immediately. "*My* house?"

I realize what I've said, and I sense my face reddening. "The house. Not mine."

But Ambrose doesn't seem convinced.

"I'll find them myself if you won't help me," I tell him, dumping the tray of snakeskin into the trash where it belongs.

———

The house's attic resembles something akin to the curtained backstage area of a small theater—dust-covered trunks and valises filled with heaps of old clothing, leather furniture with the cushioning ripped, antique artifacts like cobweb-gowned mirrors and coat racks.

I peer into the space, surveying the dark room with my flashlight as I close the attic hatch behind me. I dodge in between the flickers of sunlight collecting on the floor from the skylight above. I start disrobing some of the other furniture, clouds of dust exploding as I drag the covers from chairs and tables. Scanning my light beneath each one, I find nothing.

Suddenly, I notice something glittering that's been tucked away behind the leg of a large dresser. There, I find a small coil of snakeskin.

I drag it out and hold the brittle tube of glittering scales up to the light.

I drop it and the hose crumples on the floor as if it were made of wax paper.

My flashlight continues searching underneath more chairs and tables.

I come upon a stack of expensively framed canvas oil paintings leaning against the wall. I tip them out one by one, my light searching between each painting.

Suddenly, I find a small iron-buckled latch and the outline of a door hiding beneath one of the frames. I drag the pile of paintings away from the wall and uncover a small trapdoor.

There is a dim rattling sound echoing throughout the wall.

I unfasten the handle and lift the door—a wooden ladder leads down to a gaping maw of darkness below. I wince as a blast of cool air rushes up the tunnel to greet me and gently lifts my hair.

I hear another dim rattling sound.

Grabbing hold of the ladder's first rung, I swing my legs over the side of the opening and position my feet to begin their climb down the seemingly endless chute.

As I inch further down, my fingers come upon a rung draped with a coil of snakeskin.

I flick it away with disgust.

When my feet land on the last rung of the ladder and then touch the floor, I come upon a small door.

I lift the handle, and the door creaks open.

The room is as small and as uncomfortable-looking as a prison cell.

The walls are concrete. The space is well-lit thanks to the several naked light bulbs attached to piping that runs from one end of the room to the other.

I inch further inside the room and find a small table arranged with candles, silverware, a jug of water, and an assortment of non-perishables.

There is a small kitchenette equipped with all the necessary, albeit primitive, accoutrements.

In the corner of the room, I see a prehistoric-looking television set that probably once displayed the very first broadcast of the Moon landing. Facing the TV is a well-worn leather armchair and a matching footstool.

My nostrils flare and my face sours at a sickening smell. I look down and find a round hole cut in the concrete floor for waste. Covering my mouth and nose, I move away.

My eyes are immediately captivated by the walls dressed with an arrangement of unusual yet captivating drawings.

Although the sketches are somewhat rudimentary and look as though they were done by a child, I'm fascinated by them.

I see a drawing of the grandfather clock that once stood in the grand foyer. I scan the wall and find a sketch of a small bird perched a windowsill. Finally, I arrive at the end of the display and recognize a crude sketch of my father.

I remove the sketch from the wall, intently studying it. I regard the signature in the bottom right-hand corner of the page and frown, unable to recognize the writing.

I notice a small door on the other side of the room. It's unusually tiny and looks as though it could only lead to a cupboard.

I try the handle. Locked.

I turn and come to the center of the room, finding a small bed dressed with expensive linens.

I hold one of the pillows to my nose and deeply inhale. The smell reminds me of my father.

I close my eyes, savoring the scent.

When my eyes open, I recognize something.

I can hardly believe it.

There, abandoned on the small table beside the bed, is my precious music box.

I clear the catch in my throat, eyes shimmering wet, as I hold the box. My fingers twist the key-crank, and the lid gently lifts as the swan rotates and the waltz begins to play.

I shut my eyes again, holding the small box against my heart as I listen to the teeth of the steel comb inside being gently plucked.

I draw in a labored breath, the entire room seeming to slow with a steady pulse around me.

Just then, my fingers quiver and I send the music box crashing to the ground. The lid smashes and the swan is beheaded.

"No," I cry out.

I'm on my hands and knees in a matter of seconds, groping for the shattered remains. I cup the swan's decapitated head in my hand, and I cover my mouth at the horrible realization.

"No."

Without warning, a young girl's mouth appears in the small square-shaped opening that's been cut out of the bed's wooden paneling.

Her voice is hoarse, and she speaks as though her throat were filled with gravel.

"Pl-ease," she says. "H-help m-e."

I scream, recoiling at the sight. I crawl away until I'm huddled against the wall, my heart hammering inside my chest and my mouth open in disbelief.

The young girl's mouth puckers through the small opening, her blistered lips flexing with more intent this time.

"D-don't l-leave."

I scream, leaping from the floor.

As I escape, my careless foot catches one of the table's legs and the table capsizes. The silverware and cans fly, crashing and scattering to the floor.

One of the overturned table legs stabs my foot and I

squeal in pain as I hobble toward the door, hollering like a wounded animal.

The bunker's door flings open, and my hands are on the ladder in seconds as I begin to climb.

After scaling the ladder, I surface in the attic and throw my entire weight onto the floor. My wounded leg paining me, I hobble from one end of the attic to the other. Once I open the door, I begin lowering myself down.

However, my careless footing costs me dearly and I fall into the empty hallway.

I land with a thud on the floor, the remains of the music box still clenched in my fist.

I rake my head back, exhaling violently at my pained leg.

I try to steady my breathing.

As Ambrose comes upon me with sincere caution, he seems to immediately notice the music box in my hand.

"You found it," he says.

I shake my head at him. "Something else."

"Oh?" he says.

I pause, studying him, as if contemplating whether to tell him or not.

I reach inside my pocket and hold my hand over Ambrose's, dropping a coil of snakeskin into his open palm.

———

I watch through the door as my mother's chest rises and falls, her bedside company of machines laboring a dim hum while she sleeps.

After a moment, I close the door and I hobble back out into the hall.

I'm already lowering the attic door when my phone vibrates with a new text message.

Leaping into the air at the noise, I look at the screen and I see the contact name: Pia.

I huddle against the wall, my fingers gliding across the screen to answer.

I read the text: "Please answer, J. I just want to make things right."

I don't hesitate this time. I immediately delete the text and make my way up the ladder and crawl into the attic.

———

The light of my flashlight enters the bunker before I do. At first I'm too scared, too cautious to cross over the threshold.

Inching further inside the small room, my eyes remain fixed on the bed.

I wet my lips, my breath whistling as I slowly approach.

"Hello—?"

Crouching beside the bed, my flashlight scans underneath it until the light comes upon the small opening.

My breath is ragged and heavy when I speak.

"Are you—there?"

As I shine my flashlight through the small opening, the light comes upon the young girl's mouth.

She squirms inside the box like a pinned rat.

"W-where is he?" she asks me, trembling.

"Who—?" I ask.

"The man f-from upstairs."

My stomach curls. *She can't possibly be talking about my father*, I think to myself.

I straighten from kneeling, wincing as I lift myself up and add pressure to my wounded leg. Summoning all my strength, I begin to heave the mattress off the bed.

When I'm finished, I can see a large, beautifully ornate cedar box hidden inside the bed's framework.

The intricately built coffin-shaped trunk is not unlike a magician's disappearing box. It has a glass window fixed prominently at the center of it to showcase the person inside. There are also small, round openings where the person's hands would naturally be.

The young girl's waxen face stares back at me through the glass.

I cover my mouth, horrified at the gruesome sight—the young girl's eyes bulging from their hollowed sockets, the thinnest layer of skin stretched across pointed cheekbones, a frowning mouth with lips so chapped they appear as if they are an untreated scar.

I try to pull open the lid, but there is a lock fastened to the handle.

"I can't open it," I tell her. "Is there a key?"

The young girl's eyes are empty when she speaks. Her throat rattles the whisper of merely one word.

"B-box," she says.

I don't understand at first. I lean in closer.

"M-music—b-box."

I soon realize what she's saying.

Dipping my fingers into my pocket, I pull out the shattered remains of the music box. I unfasten the key from the crank and plug it into the coffin's latch.

The lock does not open.

As I slide the music box back into my pocket, I hear something rattle gently inside.

Fishing it back out, I lift the lid and inspect the miniature stage. It's then that I notice the stage is slanted, its edge puckering along the rim of the box and beginning to lift.

When I do, the stage rises to reveal a small golden key.

I'm on my feet again in a matter of seconds, pushing the key inside the latch and unfastening the lock.

The trunk's lid opens and finally reveals the young girl in such gruesome glory that I nearly retch at the awful sight.

She's perhaps eighteen but appears much more infant-like with her shaved head. She's gowned in a dirtied pink party dress about two sizes too small that looks somewhat familiar to me.

The place between her legs appears damp and has dried brown from uncleaned menstrual blood. Each of her fingernails is worn down to a shining, blistered nub of tissue. Her knees are bruised with giant purple welts from their uncomfortable permanent pose.

She lifts her head back, eyelids narrowing and her palsied limbs drooping as if far too exhausted to move.

I wrap my arms around the young girl's shoulders, and I gently drag her out of the coffin.

As I do, a dead rattlesnake flops out from between her

arms where it had built a small nest.

I heave her body onto the floor like a netted trout and slam the casket's lid shut.

The young girl shudders violently as if in the agonizing throes of a grand mal seizure, lips moving frantically with muted words.

I grab a nearby glass that was overturned with the kitchen table and run it under the kitchenette's faucet.

I bring the cup to her lips, and she drinks, gently swallowing at first and then suddenly with unrestrained urgency.

Downing cup after cup, she nearly chokes.

The young girl, water leaking from between her lips, looks blankly at me like a disgraced child who's just soiled their diaper.

"I n-need to be c-cleaned," she tells me.

Almost instinctively, the young girl turns for me to begin undressing her.

I unbutton her dress, revealing her backside pockmarked with needle-thin shavings of wood and blackened, belt-shaped scars of rusted blood.

I find a rag and I soak it with water, pressing the cloth against her back.

She flinches at my touch, moaning.

"Sorry," I say to her.

I continue to dab the cloth, the young girl's skin reddening at the warmth.

Then I begin to remove the splinters.

Fingers pinching the tip of the wood shaving, I slowly drag the needle out until a bead of blood drools in its place.

I dab her gently with the warm cloth.

I begin working on another splinter—this one far thicker and deeper.

Grasping the end, I start to pull. She flinches in agony, her eyes watering.

I hesitate to finish.

My resolve returning for one final pull, I drag the needle out and a jet of blood trickles from the pinhole.

The young girl cries out as I dab the cloth around the open wound, our arms wrapped around one another and feeling as if we might never let go.

———

I bring her some food from the kitchenette and watch her as she eats.

The young girl crouches on the overturned mattress, picking at a stale loaf of bread with trembling, dirt-caked fingers as she then stuffs each piece into her mouth.

I merely watch, wincing occasionally at the guttural and gurgling noises the young girl makes as she eats.

"Good?" I ask her.

The young girl merely nods, her mouth too full to answer me.

"It was all I could find in the kitchen," I tell her.

The young girl continues to gorge, ripping off bits from the heel of bread the same way a Neanderthal might have stripped meat from a carcass.

Then, as if remembering a terrible dream, the young

girl lifts her head from eating and stares at me with the utmost concern.

"He d-didn't c-come back for m-me," she says.

I straighten as she speaks.

"Who?" I ask her.

"The—m-man from upstairs," the young girl says.

I'm quiet for a moment, trying to comprehend.

"W-here is he—?" she asks me.

I do not answer. For some inexplicable reason, I'm entranced by the young girl.

"H-he said he'd always c-c-come back for me," she tells me.

"What's your name?" I ask.

The young girl's eyes dim with vacancy, her lip pulling downward.

I lean closer. I ask softly this time.

"Please," I say. "Can you tell me your name?"

Our eyes meet.

"He w-would call me J-Jay," she says. "Like the b-bird."

I can feel my face softening.

"That's my name," I tell her. "Short for Jillian."

"That's the only n-name he ever c-called me," Jay says.

"Is that not your name?"

Jay looks off, eyes searching for an answer that does not seem to exist.

"I—d-don't know," she says.

I'm without words for a moment.

"How long have you been here?"

"I'm eighteen," she tells me.

"No. Here."

Jay's lips move with soundless words at first, thinking.

"Since I was very small... Since b-before he had to w-wash the red flower e-every month."

I squint, a little bewildered by her answer. "The—red flower?"

"The one that b-bleeds between my legs," she tells me. "That was my b-birthday present when I turned twelve."

My eyes lower, understanding.

"I—learned about that from the gym teacher at boarding school," I tell her.

But Jay looks at me, confused.

"And before that—?" I ask her.

Jay shakes her head. "I—d-don't remember."

"What about your family?"

"He t-told me I had no family," she says. "Nobody wanted me."

I straighten from sitting, hooking my arm underneath Jay's to pull her up. But Jay recoils at the touch.

"What are you d-doing?" she asks me.

"Taking you out of here."

She looks around the room, nervous. "What if he comes back?"

"You weren't allowed to leave?"

"Once he let me," Jay says, her face seeming to soften at the pleasant memory. "On my thirteenth b-birthday. He took me upstairs to eat cake. That's when I hid a note in a large c-cupboard. Is that how you found me?"

I fish inside my pocket and pull out the note I had found. I unfold it in front of Jay, holding the writing up to her.

"This—?"

Jay drags the paper from my hand, reading it. A breath bottling in her throat for what seems like centuries is finally expelled.

"You f-found it. I knew s-someone would."

Jay's eyes return to me.

"C-can I—ask you something?"

I merely nod.

"Is he—dead?"

I clear the catch in my throat, eyes lowering.

"Yeah," I say, the sound of my voice thinning to a whisper. "He is."

The words settle over the quiet room like a cloud from a passing rainstorm.

Jay's face does not show expression at first.

Then she crushes the paper in her fists.

"G-good," she says. "I waited for him to d-die. I p-prayed for it every night he slept on the bed above me."

I straighten and I can sense my voice firming. "He was—"

I close my mouth before I can finish with, "my father."

Jay finishes the sentence for me instead.

"A monster," she says.

"No," I tell her.

"N-no—?"

I'm silent. I open and close my eyes, counting each breath.

"If he was a monster, then so am I."

Jay's face shows dread, as if understanding what I'm telling her.

For a moment, I'm distracted by the drawings hanging on the walls.

"He—drew with you?" I ask her.

She nods. "Every day."

"There must be a reason why he kept you down here," I say, ambling toward the wall and ripping the drawings apart as I pass each one.

"The world isn't kind to young things," I tell her. "Especially young girls. It wants to keep us as small as possible. In tiny boxes to be buried. At least here he could take care of you. That's all he was doing. Taking care of you before the world could."

My fingers brandish the key to the trunk.

"I think that's what he would want me to do, too," I tell her.

Jay's mouth is open, trying to understand. Her breath is shallow.

"It's time for bed," I say to her.

Jay shrinks, coveting the small loaf of bread, as I glower at her like a nocturnal predator that has finally caught its prey.

I push Jay back toward the casket and force her inside. She obeys my command without much resistance.

When she's lying inside, I close the lid to the trunk and my keys are already at work to fasten the lock.

I stand over the small window arranged at the center of the box, admiring my prisoner inside.

Jay, eyes glistening, stares back at me as she squirms uncomfortably.

"I-I'm still h-hungry," she says.

"I'll bring you more tomorrow," I promise her, slipping the key into my pocket.

I gather the damaged but still working music box and set it on the small table beside the trunk.

I plug the key into the crank.

Although the lid has been removed, the melody still plays. This time, however, the sound is warped and exaggeratedly out of tune.

When I'm finished listening to the waltz, I toss a white sheet across the trunk to cover Jay's dread-filled face staring back at me from the small window fixed in the center of the casket.

I meander away from my prisoner and make my way toward the bunker's small door. I'm about to leave when I turn back to face Jay one last time.

"God, I wish I could've had everything you had," I tell her.

And with that, I leave, the door closing behind me with a vulgar thud like the door to a small tomb.

The keys tightening the lock rattle violently like the beads on a rattlesnake's tail.

OCTOBER 20, 2021

I'm desperately struggling to score and slice open a fresh pomegranate with a knife. After several attempts and hardly any progress, I toss the knife aside.

Taking hold of a wooden mallet, I slam it down and the fruit explodes open with a wet squishing sound.

I begin picking the seeds out and throwing them in a small glass bowl filled with heated water.

I'm stirring gently when suddenly I hear two voices speaking in the corridor outside the kitchen.

Wiping my hands across my apron and tossing a towel over my shoulder, I slink out of the kitchen and down the hallway.

I find Ambrose leading a short gentleman in an expensive and neatly pressed three-piece suit with matching crocodile loafers toward the front door. The man carries a black briefcase made entirely out of snakeskin.

The most ostentatious aspect of his manicured look is the fact that his pencil-thin eyebrows are dyed the same bluish gray as his thinning crown of hair.

Ambrose is boyishly smitten with him, as if he were pursuing a quarterback champion for an autograph.

"You say it won't take long?" Ambrose asks him.

"I'll have my secretary write everything up this afternoon," the gentleman says. "Then it's entirely at the bank's discretion."

I watch in silence as Ambrose holds the door open for the unannounced houseguest.

"But you don't foresee any problems?" Ambrose asks him.

"Not with a signature from the primary account holder," the gentleman tells him. "The funds should be available by the weekend at the latest."

Just as the man is about to step over the threshold and leave, I call out to Ambrose.

He turns toward me, cheeks heating with embarrassment like a child that's just been caught.

"You're—up so early?" he asks me.

I inch toward the both of them.

"Who is this?" I ask Ambrose.

The gentleman extends his hand.

"Johnathan Miltner," he says.

"Your mother's attorney," Ambrose tells me.

"Pleased to meet you," Mr. Miltner says, flashing a smile of yellow teeth at me.

I approach him the same way a farmhand might approach a wolf caught in the henhouse.

"What's this about?" I ask.

Mr. Miltner stammers, unsure. He glances at Ambrose. "Your mother asked me to—"

"A personal matter," Ambrose says, interrupting.

Ambrose seethes with impatience. If he could toss Mr. Miltner out the door, he looks as though he would.

"I'm her daughter," I tell him.

"I'm afraid Mr. Miltner can't stay," Ambrose tells me. "He's already late for another appointment."

Ambrose elbows Mr. Miltner toward the open door.

"I'm very sorry for your loss, Miss Finch," Mr. Miltner says to me.

I wince a little. Apologies have always been worthless to me, especially from strangers.

"Thank you again for everything, John," Ambrose says.

"I'll be in touch."

Mr. Miltner exchanges a handshake with Ambrose before ducking out, the door shutting behind him as he leaves.

But Ambrose's swiftness can't save him from my interrogation.

"Please tell me you already started heating up her tea," Ambrose says.

"Why was he here?" I ask.

"Your mother asked for him," he tells me.

Ambrose slips past me, heading for the stairs.

"That's a lie," I say, chasing after him.

Ambrose's face hardens with anger. He loathes the fact he's been caught. He stands right at my face. An invitation for a fight.

"What would you have me tell you?" he asks me.

"What are you making her do for you?"

"Nothing she wouldn't do on her own," he says.

"You're asking me to believe that?" I ask.

"I'm not asking you to believe anything," Ambrose says, folding his arms. "You're not even supposed to be here."

"How much?" I ask.

"How much what?"

"Money," I say.

Ambrose tiptoes further up the stairs, as if attempting to escape. "I thought you didn't care about that."

"I do when it's stealing from my father," I tell him.

"You were supposed to be gone by now," he says.

I'm quiet only for a moment. My voice responds before I can actually make up my mind.

"I'm not leaving," I tell Ambrose. "Not until I find out what happened to my father."

I turn away from Ambrose, walking back to the kitchen door.

"You saw the coroner's report," he shouts at me.

"Fuck the coroner's report," I say to him. "And you."

I slip back into the kitchen and stab a pomegranate with the knife. For the first time in my life, I begin to entertain truly violent thoughts—thoughts that frighten me and make me wonder what I'm capable of doing to another living thing.

———

Later that afternoon, I visit my mother when she's finally awake from her morphine nap.

She glares at me, seemingly incredulous that I'm still present. I watch her as she straightens from her throne, the monitors beside her bed chirping whenever she exerts any movement.

"I thought you left me," she says. "I didn't think you were going to stay."

"I have to wait to get my car windshield fixed," I remind her. "The repair guy's coming to the house soon."

My mother's face seems to sour at the reminder that I'll be leaving her.

I don't have the time or the will to be poetic about the whole ordeal. I know I must confront her immediately.

"What have you done for Ambrose?" I ask her.

She gawks at me, uncertain. "Done for Ambrose?"

"Have you signed any accounts over into his name?" I ask. "Are you giving him money regularly?"

My mother shakes her head, obviously incensed I would even be bold enough to ask. "You think that's any of your business, Jay bird? Ambrose has done so much for me and your father. It's the very least we can do to repay him for his kindness."

"He's stealing from you," I tell her. "He's going to bleed you dry."

"After all he's done, he deserves some reward," my mother tells me. "Especially after all the care he provided me when the baby—"

But she stops short, severing the sentence completely.

I glare at my mother, begging her to finish what she was saying. "What baby?"

My mother closes her eyes, as if searching her mind for the right words to say.

"The baby I lost nearly twenty years ago," she whispers to me, lowering her head as if humiliated, as if truly disgraced.

I collapse on the edge of her bed, my knees buckling when she speaks.

"We didn't tell you because it was too painful at the time," my mother says. "We always wanted to keep things pleasant. The pain was too much for us to bear."

For the first time in my life, my mother resembles the vague form of something uniquely human.

"I'm sorry," I tell her.

"Ambrose was there for me when that happened," she says. "He was there when nobody else was."

I sense my hands tightening to fists. "Because you sent me away."

My mother straightens in bed, leaning forward as if to say, "Speak up."

"I could've done all I could to help you, to be a loving daughter. But you sent me away," I remind her. "You cut me off."

My mother is quiet for a moment, obviously reflecting on the ordeal, on the torment and misery she caused me.

"You're right," she says softly.

My eyes narrow at her, wondering if I've perhaps misheard. *Surely she can't be serious*, I think to myself.

"I never wanted to send you away," my mother tells me.

"That's a lie," I tell her.

"Believe what you want," she says. "I'm hoping we can start again."

I let silence settle over the room for a moment as I consider my options. Naturally, I could tell her about the young girl I've found in the bunker, or I could tell her about Ambrose's nefarious dealings. But, for some reason, I don't. I know exactly what I want—I want the house to myself.

"We can start again," I tell her. "On one condition. Let Ambrose go."

"Let go of Ambrose?" she asks me.

"Let me take care of you," I say, reaching out to touch her and offering a semblance of affection. "I want to do it."

"Ambrose has done so much for us," my mother reminds me.

"Don't you want the two of us to start again?" I ask her.

My mother's eyes lower as she considers for a moment.

"You promise you'll stay?" she asks me.

"I promise," I tell her.

It feels unusual to hold her hand. Her skin feels rough and coarse against mine as if I were touching the tail of an alligator.

I wince a little as she squeezes my hand tight.

All I can think about is how marvelously divine it will

finally feel to serve Ambrose his termination papers, to send him to pack his belongings, to watch him abandon this house forever until we're all alone here—the three of us.

———

After I swipe some provisions from the kitchen, I make my way to the attic and begin my climb down the chute toward the small bunker. When I arrive, I find Jay exactly where I left her—trapped inside the trunk like a magician's reluctant assistant.

She regards me with hopeful and yet resentful eyes, as if for the first time somewhat envious of my freedom, my ability to come and go as I please.

She wants the same thing. All caged creatures do.

I wave the loaf of bread at her so she can see. "I brought more food for you."

She's not as excited as I had hoped, however. Her eyes lower, as if disgraced.

"I need to go to the bathroom," she tells me.

Naturally, I had expected the time would come when she would need to relieve herself. I cringe at the idea of helping her, though. Why should it disgust me? *It's what my father would have done to help her*, I think to myself.

I push the key into the trunk's lock and undo the latch until the small door opens and Jay is revealed to me in all her grotesque glory. She struggles to lift herself out of the casket, so I must help her and pull her from her tiny prison.

I hook my arm around her shoulder and together we

amble toward the small opening in the floor that's been arranged for waste.

"Can you manage?" I ask her, motioning to her clothes.

Jay shakes her head, obviously embarrassed.

I pull down her underwear until she's fully exposed to me. Then I coax her to sit down over the hole in the floor so she can relieve herself. She does.

I look away out of politeness when I hear the pitter-patter while she urinates. She squats there like a bullfrog for a moment, as if thinking.

"Jillian," she says to me.

I turn to her.

"Th-there's something I-I need to t-tell you," she whispers.

I lean in close to her.

"Something I haven't t-told you," she says. "S-something you should know."

"What is it?" I ask her.

Jay looks at me like a virgin martyr about to be led to public execution.

"I killed him," she says.

I think perhaps I've misheard her. Surely, she couldn't have meant that she truly killed my beloved father. I stare at her, begging her for an explanation.

"What—?"

"The rattlesnake you discovered in my box when you first found me," she says. "I surprised him with it one night and it bit him. I watched him as he died."

I can scarcely believe what she's saying.

"You—killed him?"

Jay's eyes well with tears. "He said he was going to kill me. I had to do it."

I regard her with such bewilderment, such confusion. "You're the reason he died—?"

Jay hoists her pants around her waist and then crouches on the floor near the opening in the floor for waste.

"When it was over, I tried to leave," she explains. "But the other man from upstairs wouldn't let me. He put me back in the trunk and moved your father's body."

I shake my head in disbelief. "The other man from upstairs?"

"The one with shoes like snakeskin," Jay says. "He's kind of handsome."

I immediately know who she's talking about—Ambrose.

But it can't be, I think to myself. *Ambrose couldn't have known about this. Could he?*

"Ambrose knew you were here this whole time?" I ask her.

"He used to feed me from time to time when your father couldn't visit me," Jay explains. "I've known him all my life. He helped take care of me when I was very small. But I haven't seen him since the night your father died. I thought he was going to leave me here until I starved."

Before Jay can utter another word, I'm helping her back to the trunk and ordering her to climb inside.

"You're going to come back for me?" she asks, concerned.

But I don't make her any promises.

I ease her into the trunk and fasten the latch until I hear it click. When she's back in her place, I pocket the key and I make my way out of the bunker and back up the chute toward the attic.

I roam the corridors, calling for Ambrose.

Finally, he appears to me in the doorway leading to my mother's bedroom. He's carrying a small empty oxygen tank.

"She's sleeping," he whispers to me.

I do not hesitate. There's no room for poetry this time.

"You knew about the girl in the bunker?" I ask him.

I notice his eyes widening, his face paling. He closes the door behind him, as if to make certain my mother will not hear.

"Let's go downstairs to discuss this," he says, looping his arm around mine and guiding me further down the hall.

"No," I say, slipping out of his grasp. "I want you to tell me what you know, now."

"You're only going to upset your mother," he tells me.

"Maybe I should go tell my mother everything you seem to know," I say to him.

"It would kill her," he says.

I glance at him, uncertain what he means.

"It would kill her to know that the child she thought had died at birth was alive this whole time."

I can hardly believe what he's saying.

"Child—?"

Ambrose seems to unstiffen, finally realizing he's been caught. "Your father kept it from your mother. Because he wanted the poor thing all to himself. Just like he wanted you all to himself before your mother sent you away. She knew what he was. A monster."

I shake my head. "That's not true."

It can't be true, I think to myself. *My father wasn't a monster. Not like me.*

"He paid me an allowance every week to make certain his secret was kept," Ambrose tells me. "There. Are you happy now?"

"I know you're stealing from my mother," I tell him.

Ambrose's face heats red. "I'm only taking what I'm owed."

"I'm telling my mother," I say to him. "I think this whole thing was your idea. You kept her down there for your own sick amusement. Didn't you?"

But Ambrose doesn't answer. Instead, he's glancing down at the oxygen tank he's been holding.

I swallow nervously, moving toward my mother's bedroom door. I'm about to turn the handle when I feel something crash against the corner of my head. Stars shimmer at the edges of my vision and everything seems to blur before darkness finally claims me.

———

I awaken to the gentle *drip, drip, drip* of what feels like water on my face.

My eyelids struggle to open, and it takes me a few moments to realize where I am—deep inside the pyramid of junked furniture.

I look upward and notice the eye of the open skylight in the center of the mountain gazing down on me as if it were the eyeball of an ancient deity on fire. Glittering pellets of rainwater drip in the thin stem of the light.

I roll onto my side and notice that Jay's body has been

dumped beside me. Her head greased with blood as black as motor oil. I grab her arm and shake forcefully, begging her to wake up. But she doesn't.

Just then, I hear the dim sound of Ambrose humming.

I peer through the jungle of wasted furniture and I find Ambrose skirting around the perimeter of the mountain. He's carrying a canister of gasoline and sprinkling the area. Then, when he's satisfied with his work, he plucks a small matchbook from his pocket. I don't have to wait for him to light the match before I realize what he's going to do.

I make my way back toward Jay and I shake her. Violently, this time.

She shudders a little like a sleeping animal, her eyes opening and closing as if she were drifting in and out of consciousness. I don't have time to wait for her. I begin dragging her through the thicket of scrapped furniture, legs of armoires and ledges of credenzas stabbing me as I pass through. As I drag Jay beneath the canopy of wood, I catch sight of a long wooden rod staring at me with a tip that's been whittled to a fine point.

I snap the rod in half and carry it with me as I crawl toward safety with Jay tucked beneath my arm.

It's then I begin to smell smoke, the distant crackle of fire as Ambrose tosses more matches onto the mountain to let the whole thing burn.

I crawl faster, dodging debris and keeping Jay close.

Finally, we emerge from beneath the mountain, and I dump Jay's unconscious body on the lawn. I glance back at the pyramid of furniture and notice a curtain of fire creeping up the side of the mountain, wood blackening and narrowing to mere bits as the flames fan out further.

I peer around the corner of the mountain as it burns, and I look for Ambrose. He's nowhere in sight.

I'm about to return to Jay and drag her back to the house when Ambrose grabs me, squealing like swine about to be executed and clawing at me. He wraps his hands around my throat and begins to squeeze tight. But I remember that I'm still holding the wooden spear. I knock him over the head with it and he staggers back for a moment, his eyes searching mine.

He's not down for long, however.

Ambrose rushes toward me one final time. However, he meets the tapered end of my spear before he can reach me. I slide the rod into his stomach and twist it—hoping it pains him, hoping it pierces the black root sprouting deep inside him. He halts, as if some invisible hand has commanded him to do so. He gazes at me with childlike curiosity—as if surprised, as if unsure of what had just happened. It's then I notice blood drooling from the corners of his mouth.

He does not resist or swipe at me as I had imagined he might. I drag the spear from his gut, and I watch him as he clutches his wounded stomach, his shirt dyed dark red as more blood blooms there like a flower. I watch in silence as Ambrose staggers back, his lips moving with muted condemnations. There's nothing I can do to help him. In fact, there's nothing I want to do to help him. There's a quiet, curious part of me that wants to watch him die.

Finally, he does.

He curls on the ground like a dying insect, and I watch as more blood leaks from the hole I've opened in his stomach until a dark tide leaches across the lawn.

When I'm certain Ambrose is dead, I limp toward Jay. She greets me with open eyes. Bewildered, confused.

I wrap my arm around her shoulder and drag her toward the house. We turn occasionally to watch the mountain of furniture burn. But a voice fills my head and tells me to keep moving forward.

A snake doesn't glance back and think to itself, "This skin was once mine," the voice tells me. *A snake always moves forward.*

So that's exactly what I do.

I keep moving forward until the crackling sounds of the inferno are but a distant memory, until they're smeared from my thoughts completely and I am washed clean of the soot and smoke.

———

Jay and I arrive in the entryway of the house. I ease Jay into a nearby chair and I survey the area, dropping the wooden spear and letting it clatter on the floor.

"What are we going to do?" Jay asks me.

At first, I'm unsure. I don't know what to do. I certainly can't call the police and tell them what happened. All I can do is return to the pyramid later and hope most of Ambrose's body has been burned.

"We're going to get you cleaned up," I tell Jay, smearing

some of the blood from the open wound in her head. "Then we're going to bring you back to the bunker."

Jay looks at me, incredulous. "Back to the bunker—?"

"That's where my father would have wanted you to stay," I tell her. "That's where I'll take care of you."

I cup Jay's cheek, but she recoils at the slightest hint of my touch.

"What's the matter?" I ask her.

Jay swallows nervously, lifting herself out of the chair. "I don't want to go back to that place. Can't I stay here with you?"

I shake my head. "It's not what my father would have wanted."

Just then, I notice Jay's eyes coveting the wooden spear I had discarded on the floor. Before I can swipe it, she's already grabbing it. I shrink from her, but it's too late. She drives the tip of the spear into my shoulder until I'm impaled.

I heave as she stirs the rod in its place. My vision becomes hazy again, my knees quivering and threatening to give out completely. I'm on the marble floor in a matter of seconds. It feels as though my very soul is unraveling, as if Jay has undone the very essence of my being and is unspooling me bit by bit until I am nothing more than a mere stain.

After all I have done to her, I realize that it's what I truly deserve.

———

I awaken and find my arms pinned at my sides. There's a small window I can see through, but the view isn't much.

From my little window, I notice Jay milling about in the corner of the bunker.

"Jay," I say to her. "What are you doing? Let me out."

But she won't listen to me.

"Please," I beg her. "Don't do this."

Jay turns gently and approaches me while I shift uncomfortably inside the small trunk, tiny slivers of wood spearing me.

"This is what love is," she tells me. "That's what he taught me."

I realize that it's probably futile to reason with her, but I try to, anyway.

"Jay, there are going to be people looking for me," I explain to her. "They're going to come here. My mother will wonder where I've gone."

"Don't worry," she tells me. "I'll take care of you. Just like you took care of me when I needed you most."

With trembling hands, Jay passes bits of bread through the small window. At first, I'm hesitant. But I cannot deny the fact that I'm starving. I begin to feed, and it looks as though for the very first time Jay is pleased with me, as if she's delighted to finally take care of something, as if this is what she was truly always meant to do.

Finally, I tell her something that I think I've perhaps known since the moment I first met her, since I first found her and decided to keep her the way my father had once kept her.

"I'm your sister, Jay," I say to her.

She looks at me queerly, as if I were speaking some ancient dialect.

"You could do this to your own sister?" I ask.

Jay thinks for a moment, wondering if she's capable of following through with her designs. She closes her eyes, clearing the catch in her throat.

"Sometimes to heal, you must hurt something," she tells me, passing more bits of food through the window and into my open mouth.

I don't have to ask her where she learned that.

OCTOBER 25, 2021

Days pass and Jay routinely checks on me as I rest inside the small trunk. She brings me scraps of food from the kitchenette and occasionally positions the television set in such a way that I can watch a program for half an hour or so.

I've stopped begging for her to release me. I know for certain that day will never come.

She doesn't even allow me to use the small hole in the floor where the waste collects. She says she's afraid of what I might try to do if I were ever freed from the trunk. She says that she's afraid I'll hurt her, afraid I'll do something worse to her.

I tell her it's only natural to hurt the things we love the most.

I curse myself for telling her something so senseless. I wonder if she'll eventually kill me—if she'll spear me again or if she'll simply leave me here to starve to death.

But then I remember that the worst thing a person can do to you after they've hurt you is let you live.

That's how you truly and unmistakably destroy another human being.

I can tell for certain that's what she wants. That's what she's been waiting for and that's what I deserve, after all.

She's going to let me live.

SEEDLING

"Any life is made up of a single moment, the moment in which a man finds out, once and for all, who he is."

Jorge Luis Borges

It was nearly five a.m. on a Wednesday morning when my father called to tell me that my mother had died.

Of course, I had been expecting the cheerlessness of his tone to greet me on the other end of the line with unfortunate news for quite some time; however, I certainly had never expected his voice to break apart like damp tissue paper while he sobbed, the words seeming to choke him all at once.

It felt peculiar—perhaps even decidedly wrong—to listen to my father weep so openly, to hear the tattered murmur of his breathing while he labored with each and every syllable. While he struggled to speak, I searched my mind for a recollection of a moment when we were so vulnerable, so remarkably exposed to one another. I could think of none.

For as long as I could remember, my father and I had spent year after year torturing ourselves on either side of an invisible gate that seemed to eternally separate us. Of course, there were times—few and far between—when one of us would open the postern slightly and peer across the threshold. Those moments were short-lived, however, and usually would end with us not speaking to one another for months at a time.

In fact, it was my mother who had kept us together. If it weren't for her grace, her carefulness, her dedication, my father and I would have gone our separate ways and left the invisible gate closed and latched forever. Of course, that wasn't to say there was any semblance of animosity lingering between us. Still, there were moments when I considered securing the invisible doorway between us so that neither one of us could pass through to the other.

While my father wept, I entertained those thoughts once more. For a man who seemed to struggle to congratulate me with even a handshake after any modicum of success, it seemed so particularly unlike him to expose himself so fully and so unreservedly to me.

Once he had finished sharing the more unsavory details of my mother's passing with me, I told him I would get dressed and head over to the house at once.

"I—didn't expect you to come over right away," he said, his voice trembling a little. "I just wanted you to know."

In my peripheral vision, I noticed my husband, Clive, stirring beneath the sheets. He stretched, yawning, and rubbed his eyes slightly to clear the crust from the corners.

"Are you there by yourself?" I asked my father, for once concerned for him.

I was loath to think of him remaining in the house—milling about from room to room like a shapeless specter—while my mother's body languished and rotted away by the seconds in the nearby bedroom. To me, it was far too ghoulish a thought.

"The hospice nurses are still here," he told me. "They have a few things to tend to."

It felt so strange hearing my father describe my mother's demise as something that others would need to "tend to," as if she were now nothing more than a house plant.

Is that what we become? I wondered to myself. *Useless vegetation that would rot if we didn't have others to tend to us?*

After I told my father I would dress and head over, I hung up the phone and sat on the edge of the bed for what felt like hours even though it was most likely only a few minutes. I wasn't alone for long, as Clive eventually straightened and pushed all his weight against me. He glanced at the clock and then groaned.

"It's five in the morning," he said. "Why are you up?"

Part of me wondered if I should tell him—if I should reveal the horrible news right away or let him rest a little while longer. But I knew full well how there was some unnamable urge rooted in every human being that compelled us to drag others into our suffering, our despair.

"It's bad news," I told him.

Out of the corner of my eye, I watched him stir gently once more. He leaned against me, wrapping an arm around my shoulder, as if already seeming to know.

"Is it—?"

The remainder of his question hung in the air like a fine mist.

"My mother's dead," I said to him gently.

The words came from deep within me and surprised me a little because they were issued without emotion, without feeling.

I said it again: "My mother's dead."

Then I said it again and again, Clive pulling me closer against him as my voice began to dissolve like sugar in heated water.

I suddenly felt sick, bile pulsing from my stomach and up into my throat. I braced myself on the edge of the bed and vomited next to the bureau. Clive rubbed the small of my back, occasionally stroking my hair, until I was finished. Then he skirted into the bathroom and delivered a warm, damp towel to me so that I could clean my face.

When I scrubbed my skin, I couldn't help but think how I felt as if I would never be truly and completely clean. It suddenly felt as if I had been tainted, as if my skin had been permanently marked by all my mother had left behind.

I yearned to tell Clive what I thought—how filthy I had suddenly felt—but I reasoned that I had already polluted him enough, and I suddenly worried that there were far worse things to come.

———

Clive begged to join me, but I told him that I preferred to see my father alone for the time being.

It wasn't that I didn't want Clive present or that I didn't desperately need him. Quite the contrary. It was simply because I knew I didn't want to burden him yet with that kind of pain, that kind of suffering. After all, Clive's mother was still healthy and able to visit us on the weekends when she wasn't visiting her other son who lives in Kittery, Maine. For the first time in my life, I envied Clive. I envied the fact that he still had a mother. I resented the fact that he wasn't abandoned as an orphan.

To me, it didn't matter that I would be turning thirty next month. I still thought of myself as an orphan—some poor, pathetic thing who had been discarded and cast out to be broken by the cruelty of the world.

After an hour or so, I arrived at my parents' home. It felt peculiar to consider the small Dutch Colonial tucked away behind a grove of trees at the end of Balsam Lane as my "parents' home." I knew for a fact it wasn't any longer. It was now only my father's home.

I sat in the driveway for a few minutes, collecting my thoughts. I wondered if and when my mind would eventually stop racing.

Finally, after several minutes of debating whether or not to go inside, I peeled myself from the driver's seat and meandered up the stone pathway leading to the front door. As I strolled, I couldn't help but notice the decorative gnomes my mother had arranged throughout the small garden weaving around the front of the large house. I had always teased her and reminded her of my distaste for them. I suddenly felt myself drawn to them—as if they had finally enchanted me, as if each one was winking at me with the promise of keeping my beloved mother alive by their very presence.

I arrived at the front door and knocked twice. It wasn't long before I heard the approaching shuffle of feet pattering against hardwood floors. Finally, the door swung open and revealed my father standing there in his flannel bathrobe. He greeted me with a smile that soon began to disintegrate until he lunged forward at me, collapsing into my arms and sobbing violently. I held him for a moment, my hands unsure where to go as I found myself too uncomfortable to touch him. Eventually, I leaned into his embrace and patted him gently while he cried.

We stood on the front porch, the sounds of his sobbing echoing throughout the neighborhood as if in desperation to tell others that death had finally arrived here, and that death would be staying for quite some time.

———

After my father collected himself, we drifted from the entryway into the living room, where they had arranged my mother's makeshift bed—the place where she had spent her last few weeks of suffering. Of course, I wasn't surprised to discover a few nurses moving about the room and collecting various pieces of equipment. However, I found myself immediately shrinking from the horrible—practically gruesome—sight of my dead mother lying in the bed, her arms pinned at her sides and her eyes respectfully closed.

I sensed myself inching away, fumbling to think of an excuse to remove myself from the room at once. My father seemed to notice my hesitation.

"I thought you might want to say goodbye," he said to me, his head lowering. "I asked them to keep her here a little while longer so you could see her. Pay your last respects."

"That—wasn't necessary," I told my father, my voice threatening to tremble. "I think—I need some air."

Before my father could utter another word, I sprang from the room and into the foyer where I was sick in a small waste bucket that had been left beside the stairwell by one of the nurses. After I wiped the vomit smeared along my chin, I made my way into the kitchen, where I searched for a glass of water.

As I ran a small cup under the kitchen faucet, I noticed my father appear in the kitchen doorway. He folded his hands together as if in prayer and lowered his head.

"I—really think you should pay your last respects to your mother," he told me. "You know how much she loved you."

Yes, of course, I thought to myself. *What an insipid thing to say. I know full well how much my mother cared for me. What makes my father think I'm capable of walking up to her corpse and seeing her like this?*

I stammered, uncertain. "I suppose—I'd like to remember her as she was."

"I don't want you to regret anything," my father said to me. "When my mother died when I was your age, I made time to grieve. It takes a while. But it's necessary to do so."

Of course, I knew it would be necessary to grieve my mother and reconcile with the fact that she was gone. But I had no intention of honoring that grief today. Especially with my father present. I would instead return to the comfort of the life I had built with my beloved Clive and work through the trauma, the suffering there.

"When are they going to take her?" I asked my father.

"As soon as you say your goodbyes," he told me, folding his arms.

I felt a familiar pang of resentment as I regarded him. I recognized full well the "I know better than you" lilt of his voice. Part of me wondered why I had even come here in the first place.

"Do you have everything you need here?" I asked him, hoping I could somehow change the subject. "Will the neighbors look in on you?"

"Your mother and I don't really know many of the neighbors," he said, shuffling toward the cabinet and picking up a small cup for tea. "A lot of new families moved here."

"Do you want Clive and me to look in on you for a while?" I asked him.

There was a small, quiet part of me that hoped he might shoo me away, that he might wave me off and insist he was more than capable of caring for himself as a seventy-five-year-old man.

"I worry about staying here alone," he said to me, his eyes drifting around the room as if the house were somehow able to swallow him whole. "Especially at night."

"Should Clive and I come stay with you?" I asked him.

He wouldn't look at me, as if too fearful to admit he was frightened and desperately needed his son's help.

"Perhaps until the funeral?" he asked me. "Do you think you can manage that?"

Of course, there was a part of me that didn't want to—a selfish, spoiled part that would rather recklessly abandon my father and seek comfort in the only man who had ever made me feel like a good and decent human. But I reasoned that I couldn't abandon my father even if he had been more than absent for most of my life. He deserved better than that.

"I'll call Clive and tell him to come over," I told my father, making my way toward the kitchen door after draining the glass of water in the sink.

"What about your mother?" my father asked me. "Your last respects."

"When I come back," I promised him, skirting out of the kitchen and away from his eyesight.

I made my way out of the house and onto the front porch to search for decent cell reception. I pulled my phone from my pocket, slid my finger across the screen, and dialed Clive's number. When he answered, I told him to pack some of our things and to be ready for me when I returned in an hour so.

"How's he doing?" Clive asked me, his voice thinning and crinkling like a candy wrapper on the other end of the line.

"He's holding it together. But barely," I told him. "We might be staying here for quite some time if he needs us."

Clive exhaled. "You know I'm here for you and whatever your family needs."

"I just wish there was a way to not feel anything," I said to him. "If there was a way to move past the grief, the despair."

Clive said something, but I couldn't catch it because the line began to hiss like radio static once more.

"Sorry," I said. "Say it one more time."

Just then, the call disconnected.

I tried dialing him again, but the call went straight to his voicemail for some reason. I figured I would call him again when I was on the road.

I went back inside the house to find my father.

As I was about to close the front door, I couldn't help but notice a tiny hole—no bigger than a dime—had opened along the side of my wrist. I lifted my arm closer and noticed that the small wound seemed to reveal something black as motor oil. There was no blood. There were no signs of muscles or tendons to be exposed. Instead, there was a small pocket of darkness blistered with glittering specks of light, as if I had an eternity of distant constellations whirling inside me.

————

As I walked past the living room, I couldn't help but steal a moment to peer inside at where my mother's body remained. I found her reclining on the bed like a sleeping dowager, hospice nurses flittering about her bedside like worrisome mothers tending to a poorly child.

Yes, a child, I thought to myself.

I always found it troubling how, as my parents both aged, the more like children they seemed to become. I thought of pitiful phone conversations when my mother struggled to find the right words to describe a mere bird she had seen earlier that same day. I thought of the horrible moment when she soiled herself after dinner one evening and I took her upstairs to clean her. Of course, I never resented her or the way in which she aged. I merely hated the fact that old age had finally robbed from her its final penance.

I thought of entering the room and loitering beside my mother's deathbed, pacing back and forth there until I could work up the courage to look at her. Perhaps even talk to her. I wasn't certain what I might say. What was there to say, after all? Perhaps I would make some senseless comment about the weather or pretend as if she could answer my burning inquiries about her health. I thought that maybe if I became comfortable enough with the fact that she was very much gone, perhaps I could work up enough bravery to touch her one final time.

But just as I was about to cross the threshold and enter the room, my father moved beside me and startled me.

"I like to think of it as if it were a special plant," he told me with a queer matter-of-factness.

I searched him for an explanation, begging to understand what he meant.

"The cancer, I mean," he said. "It grew from a small seedling—planted there probably when she was a little girl— and took from her again and again until it finally bloomed. It's always been growing in her."

I hesitated slightly, not sure if his analogy comforted me or if it upset me even more. After all, to think of something flowering deep inside my mother and robbing her of all her joy, cheeriness, and vitality seemed unbearable. If the cancer that took her from us was anything it was a black weed—a horrible vine that pushed all of her out until there was nothing left inside.

"It's going to be difficult for things to continue with your mother now gone," he told me. "Your mother kept things together."

I glanced down, remembering the small wound I had noticed along my wrist, and found it was still there. The lips of the wound seemed to curl at me—as if threatening to part further, as if impatient to reveal more of the black licorice-looking sinew beneath.

"Do you have a first-aid kit?" I asked my father, hiding the small wound from him, fearful it might upset him. "I think I cut myself on something."

After my father led me to the kitchen cabinet and offered the auxiliary kit from the pantry, I dressed the wound as best I could. When I was finished, I thought of how it might feel to remain in the house with my father until the funeral. Of course, Clive would be here with me, but I knew it would be more than unbearable.

"Dad, why don't you come stay with Clive and me?" I asked him. "I think you might be more comfortable there."

My father squinted at me, as if suspicious. "You don't have enough room for me there. I might as well just stay put."

I shook my head. "I don't want you staying here by yourself. Besides, the house is far too gloomy. We need to get you in better spirits. Go upstairs and pack a small bag. I'll get the car ready."

I could tell my father was going over his options in the privacy of his mind, searching for an excuse.

Finally, he agreed, and I pushed him along to head upstairs so that he could pack his suitcase.

I raced outside, my fingers swiping my phone screen to call Clive once more and let him know that my father would be staying with us for a while—at the very least until after the funeral.

But just as I stepped out onto the porch and a blast of cool autumn air hit me, I sensed my skin begin to crackle and shrink as if it could wrench itself from me at any moment and unspool in thick wisps. I glanced down and noticed another small black hole had opened in the palm of my hand. This time, the hole was the size of a quarter, and the edges were cemented black with what looked like soot or ash. I stared at the wound and once again found no blood or exposed muscle. Instead, I was met with sinew as dark and as glistening as precious onyx. I could scarcely believe it.

What the fuck is happening to me? I thought to myself as I regarded the tiny wound yawning at me in the palm of my hand.

I skirted inside the house and called for my father.

He greeted me at the top of the stairs, his suitcase in hand, and began to march down toward me when I told him that something was very wrong.

"Are you ill?" he asked me, imitating a somewhat familiar and yet obviously rehearsed father-like concern.

I merely told him to send the hospice nurses on their way so we could leave as soon as possible.

"They'll wait here until the folks from the funeral home arrive," he told me. "They don't mind."

Satisfied with the plan, I ushered him from the foot of the stairs and out the front door. He leaned against me a little too much as we drifted down the front steps and along the pathway leading toward my parked car. However, just as we neared the edge of the path, my father began to slow, as if troubled. He hesitated, his pace crawling to a stop and clutching his chest.

"Is something wrong?" I asked him. "Your heart?"

"I—feel dizzy," he told me, his head wobbling back and forth. "Can we sit down for a moment?"

Just then, I noticed something that shocked me, something that severed my tongue and cheated all possibility of words from the pit of my throat. I saw a small, glistening black wound wink at me along my father's forehead. It looked as if the skin had been wrenched open by invisible fingers, the edges around the tiny opening dimpled slightly like the honeycomb from a beehive. Inside the small opening was a familiar sight—candied oblivion, too dark and yet somehow also too shiny to draw near enough to touch.

I grabbed hold of my father's wrist, and it was then I noticed another little opening beginning to pucker at me along his liver-spot-dotted forearm. Once again, there was no blood or anything that resembled typical exposed tissue. There was merely darkness that seemed to beckon me, invite me to draw closer and try touching it.

But I didn't.

Instead, I looped my arm through my father's and hauled him back up the pathway until I delivered him inside the house. He wheezed, closing his eyes, and steadied himself against the stairwell banister as he continued to struggle to breathe.

I darted into the kitchen, poured a glass of water, and then returned to my father and begged him to drink. He did so reluctantly.

When his breathing became less ragged, I ushered him into the living room and placed him in a chair beside my mother's bed. It was then I looked around the room and realized that the hospice nurses were absent.

"The nurses left already?" I asked him.

But my father couldn't answer. His eyes were fixed on my mother's corpse, coveting her with such unrestrained longing.

Moving back into the kitchen, I located the auxiliary kit once more. I returned to my father and began to clean the wounds that had sprouted along his skin, dimpling there like tiny black lesions from a nameless plague.

I felt him wince slightly as I dabbed the affected area with a small pad of rubbing alcohol. He looked at me, distrustful, as if I secretly wanted to hurt him. I softened my gaze at him, silently telling him that I merely wanted to help.

Suddenly, something pulled my attention back to the wound winking at me from his forearm. I looked closer at the small opening and it was then that I noticed a tiny black thread—wire-like and as thin as a vine—curling from deep inside my father's wound and wrapping itself around my finger for a moment. I shuddered as the thread coiled around me, tightening a little with neither an introduction nor a threat. It wasn't long before the tiny black thread unraveled from me and then disappeared inside my father's arm like a defenseless creature that wished to hide itself from starved predators.

I sat there in amazement, studying my father's wound, and waiting for the black thread to appear to me again. Instead, the darkness residing in the small pocket of his open skin stared back at me and seemed to shimmer, as if pleased to know I was so curious.

———

After I finished dressing my father's open wounds, I asked him if he felt feverish or ill.

"I just—felt dizzy for a bit. That's all," he told me. "I think it's passed."

I lifted his wrist and showed him the small wound I had bandaged.

"Does it hurt—?" I asked him, peeling back some of the dressings and exposing the horrible black, scabbed opening beneath.

I watched him carefully as his eyes searched the wound for a moment, his lips moving with muted words as if struggling to answer me.

"What is it?" he asked.

I revealed my identical wounds to him, unwrapping some of the bandage and showing him how we were unexpectedly siblings of a similar unknown affliction.

"I don't know what it is," I said to him. "It could be some kind of—infection. It only seems to appear when I step outside. I've never seen anything like it."

I was surprised to notice that my father did not look concerned, but rather appeared to accept what I was telling him with the quiet dignity that all elderly gentlemen seem to share with regard to the inevitable. There was no panic in his eyes, no signs of desperation nor fear. He seemed to accept everything I said with a remarkable grace that I couldn't help but envy.

Just as I was about to haul him from his seat, my father straightened and drifted over toward my mother's bedside. I watched him as he took my mother's lifeless hand in his and squeezed tight, wincing a little. I saw as tears began to web in the corners of his eyes.

"Where have the nurses gone?" I asked him. "Surely they couldn't have left already."

My father merely shrugged; his eyes were fixed on my poor mother's lifeless body.

"Dad, come away from her," I said to him. "Let her be."

I grabbed my father's wrist and then sensed my hand touching some of the bandage I had prepared for him, my fingers slipping underneath the dressing and circling the rim of the wound I had covered. For a moment, I allowed my index finger to linger there, gently teasing the edges of the opening. Before I could think to pull myself away, my finger made the dreadful decision for me and slid inside the small opening.

I felt myself tense as my fingers stirred in the open socket, something whispering to me to push a little deeper inside. I obeyed without comment, pressing deeper inside the small opening, and not caring whether or not the lips of the wound would stretch further. In fact, they did. As I went deeper, I sensed the opening part further and further. I shook my head in disbelief, a warm sensation beginning to pulse throughout the entirety of my body.

Without warning, a small black tendril unspooled from deep within the wound and braided itself around my index finger the way Japanese wisteria might cling to an abandoned fence. Another one sprouted from the opening not long after, also looping itself around me. I felt myself shudder, more plant-like threads creeping out of the hole in my father's wrist and coiling around my finger.

I looked at my father and found he wasn't even paying attention to what I was doing—the wider opening I had made in his arm. Instead, he was gazing with such unreserved love at my mother's corpse. I thought to say something—to sever him from his trance—but I worried I might spoil the moment.

When the wound was finally choked with black threads as thick as electrical cables, I pulled my finger from the opening and watched as the tendrils gently unraveled from me and then retreated to safety deep inside the pocket of my father's tar-black wound. I stood there for a moment in utter amazement, a feeling not too dissimilar from joy coursing through me like livid whitewater currents.

When I finally composed myself and realized that the sensation was dimming with each and every second, I pulled myself away from my father and reeled slightly as if I had hurt him. He didn't appear damaged. In fact, he didn't appear to have even registered that I had done anything questionable to him to begin with. Instead, he sat in his chair and examined my mother's body, eyeing her with such scrutiny and longing, as if willing to somehow resurrect her.

"Let's go into the kitchen," I said, nudging his shoulder.

He leaned against me as he struggled to rise to his feet. As I steered him from the living room into the kitchen, I couldn't help but sense something deep within me urging me to do it again—to push my finger deep inside my father's open wound and search for meaning, forgiveness, even an absolution. I loathed myself for entertaining the hideous thought, but I couldn't help but wonder when I might partake again, when I might peel back the bandage and push inside him until my index finger reached his rotting core.

It would be a way to finally and completely understand him, I thought to myself. *Yes, think of it as a way to finally understand him.*

———

We arrived in the kitchen, and I helped my father to the small dining room table arranged in the corner of the room.

It felt foolish to admit, but I was frightened of stepping outside in case another wound might open. I knew I had to call Clive and let him know what was happening, but there was hardly any service inside my parents' house and they had disconnected their landline a few years ago after a series of obnoxious telemarketing calls.

I watched as my father eased himself into the chair, his limbs creaking a little as he bent. When he finally settled himself, I pulled out a chair and sat beside him. For a while we sat in silence, our eyes avoiding one another as if out of respect. Occasionally, I would glance at him and notice he was staring off, his mind very much elsewhere.

Although I detested myself for doing it, I sensed my eyes drift toward the bandage I had carefully wrapped around my father's wrist. I coveted the dressing, imagined peeling it away and slipping my finger inside the small opening again and again until more black threads flowered from their hiding places.

"I really think you should pay your last respects to your mother," my father said, pulling me from the privacy of my imagination and delivering me back to the tiny kitchen table where we sat. "You owe her that at the very least."

I sensed myself quiver, dreading the possibility of being near my mother's dead body and inhaling her vile, lifeless scent.

"I—want to remember her as she was," I told him, pulling my eyes away from him and gazing at one of the several paintings they had pinned to the kitchen wall. "I don't want to remember her like this."

"You'll never move on if you don't pay your respects," my father told me. "It's imperative."

Of course, there was a quiet part of me that knew what he was saying was true. I knew that if I didn't reconcile my grief for my dead mother, I would be haunted by all I had done to prolong the pain, to encourage the suffering. However, I couldn't be bothered with that right now. I was far too smitten, much too enraptured with the idea of indulging in my new, horrible vice: my father's open wound.

It was then I sensed the wound in my palm begin to itch. I slid my finger underneath the bandage and began to scratch the tiny opening. But the itching somehow grew worse. I could hardly bear it any longer.

I eyed my father's wound on his wrist and the horrible thought came to me once more.

"Dad, look away," I told him.

"What—?"

"Just do it," I ordered.

As soon as my father looked away from me, I tore the bandage from his wrist and exposed the glistening black wound. Without warning, dark vines crept from deep inside the corners of the opening and curled at me with an invitation. I pushed my finger inside, circling there, and then forcing myself deeper and deeper inside the wet sleeve. I couldn't help but notice how the edges of the wound began to spread further and further, his skin splitting as if it were inexpensive fabric. I realized it only too late—his skin crackling like wasted honeycomb. I thought of stopping myself, but the sensation was far too great. The pleasure was indescribable and all-consuming.

As I pushed myself in deeper—my father's wound parting further and further until my entire fist had been shoved inside—I noticed, out of the corner of my eye, my father weeping gently. He stirred there in his seat, sobbing, and keeping his eyes away from me.

I didn't feel pity for him. Instead, I felt puzzled. Why, after all this time, did he decide to fully reveal himself to me? Why did it take my mother dying for him to really and truly be himself around me?

"You never liked me," I said to him quietly, my fist working deeper and deeper inside his open wound. "There was something about me that you didn't care for."

My father laughed a little, wiping the tears from his eyes. "Is that what you think—?"

"Tell me it's not true," I said to him. "Convince me that I'm wrong."

My father merely shook his head, already seemingly defeated. "You've already made up your mind it seems."

"You made it too obvious," I told him. "You never wanted to be a father."

"I loved being a father," he said. "I loved being your father. But I knew the world wouldn't be kind to you because of what you are. The world eats away at things it doesn't understand."

I smiled, realizing he was right.

"I suppose I never really understood you," I told him.

My father cleared the catch in his throat. "I never understood you, too."

I pushed my arm inside my father's wound, the black vines crawling toward me, locking themselves around me and then dragging me deeper until my entire arm had been swallowed by them. I watched my father wince as I was pulled inside the gaping and glittering dark maw that was staring back at me.

Realizing that he would never understand me if I didn't let him in, I peeled the bandage from my hand and guided one of his trembling fingers toward my open wound. I pushed him inside and let him settle there for a moment, black threads unspooling from deep within me and clutching at him. I flinched a little, my skin parting further as he was pulled inside my wound.

It felt so decidedly unnatural—rooting around in the voids that had grown from our grief, our heartache, our despair. However, at the same time, it somehow felt so freeing to be so exposed with the father I hardly knew.

It wasn't long before his arm had been fully inhaled by the black vines creeping from my open wound. I watched his surprise, his astonishment as he was pulled deeper. I was afraid, but, for some reason, my apprehension didn't stop me from drawing closer, from shoving more of my arm inside the void glaring at me.

Before long, we collapsed into one another, a grave of black weeds choking us as we finally surrendered and drifted toward a merciful oblivion.

———

After we heaved ourselves from the wounds we had spread from one another, my father and I found ourselves thrashing against the floor like fish captured in a fisherman's net. When I finally collected myself, I noticed my father had already curled in a corner beside the counter and moored himself there. He shivered, as if frightened, when I drew closer to touch him. He seemed to tremble, as if fearful I might have a desire to go through the ordeal one more time. I petted him softly—assuring him that it was over, that our introduction to one another was finally finished.

I looked down at my palm and wrist, noticing that the wounds which were once open there and blinking constellations at me were now completely absent—as if the skin there had been closed, as if it had never been opened in the first place.

Then I urged my father to lean over, exposing himself to me, and it was then I realized that his wounds, although shrinking, were still present. I brought my fingers close to one of the wounds and it immediately seemed to pout, leaking fluid as dark as motor oil. He writhed there, convulsing violently as if bewitched by an agony I could never and would never want to understand.

When his seizure was finished, I ladled him from the floor and carried him into the living room, where I finally delivered him to my mother's bed. I arranged his trembling body beside her lifeless corpse and dragged a sheet to cover them both until they were swaddled.

I stared at my father, begging him to say something—anything.

Finally, he opened his eyes and squinted at me, as if perplexed by my presence.

"I like to think of it as if it were a special plant," he told me. "It grew from a small seedling—planted there probably when I was a little boy—and took from me again and again until it finally bloomed. It's always been growing in me. In all of us."

I watched in silence as my father's wounds shivered slightly. They opened and closed. Then vines and tar-black tendrils poured out of him like dark fluid and began to snake across my mother's lifeless body until she was finally covered, until her tiny shape had been swallowed completely and she was comfortably swaddled like a precious newborn in a bassinet.

"It's going to be difficult for things to continue with your mother now gone," my father whispered. "Your mother kept things together."

I realized he was right. What would keep us all together now she was gone? Of course, we could try to move on, could try to repair the damage we had done to one another after all these years. But it would be futile. What point was there to go on as if foolishly pretending things would always be the same?

Before another moment of hesitation, I crawled into bed beside my mother and father. My father regarded me with a distinct gentleness I hadn't seen him possess before—a tenderness that seemed to comfort and astonish me all at once.

I wrapped my arms around my mother's cooling body, drawing in her scent. My father leaned closer against her, pulling at the wound in his wrist and teasing more black threads out from their hiding places until they were zigzagging across my mother's corpse and muting her shape in a livid blur.

I did what I thought I was supposed to do. I grabbed hold of the lips of my father's wound and stretched it further and further until he collapsed into himself, until he was nothing more than a gentle whisper—something that could never be undone. I dragged the dark threads from deep inside him and poured them over my mother, drowning her—drowning the both of us until the three of us were lost together, unfettered in an endless sea where heartache and despair had no proper place, where we were nameless and shining and new and could finally be together as one.

———

When the police arrived to search my parents' home, they found my mother and father bound together in a seemingly permanent embrace, the bedsheets washed in a tide of their blood. They told me I was found kneeling on the kitchen floor, stabbing the tiles with a knife I had recovered from one of the drawers.

They said that I had been there for several days, and they plugged their noses when they came near me, as if the odor of blood cemented on my skin offended them far more than what I had actually done to my father.

From what I could piece together as they dragged me from the house, horrible things had been done to my father's body after he perished—wounds that had been forced open and stretched to their utmost limits.

They said that I did those things.

Of course, I didn't believe them.

I nearly wept when they told me how my mother's and father's bodies were so dangerously intertwined with one another that some of their limbs snapped when they attempted to pull them apart.

As I sat in the back seat of a police cruiser that idled in my parents' driveway, I sensed something pinched in the back of my throat and tickling me there. I strained to cough but could force nothing out.

I thought of what my father had said—how seedlings are planted deep within us when we're very young, and how they take from us until they can finally bloom and fully reveal themselves to us. I knew he was right. In the blackest pit of my heart, I knew my father was right.

I cleared my throat and sensed myself soften a little, waiting for the seeds set in my breath to finally bud and divulge their secrets to me.

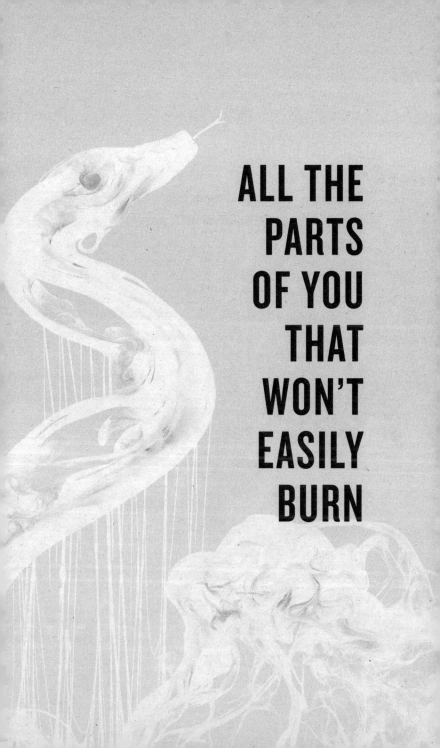

ALL THE
PARTS
OF YOU
THAT
WON'T
EASILY
BURN

"I must get my soul back from you;
I am killing my flesh without it."

Sylvia Plath

ONE

In Enoch Leadbetter's most earnest estimation, the shopkeeper is no older than forty-eight or forty-nine years old. Even though he's prematurely graying and carrying perhaps a few more extra pounds than he should considering the unimpressive shortness of his stature, he remains a captivating—yes, perhaps even beguiling—presence when he greets Enoch as soon as he passes across the threshold and rings the small bell attached to the shop's door handle.

He resembles the type of gentleman Enoch might see on a morning stroll in the park—the pensive, polite-looking man who probably collects his dog's droppings in an expensive bag from Bergdorf Goodman and obeys all proper signage when crossing the street. From what Enoch can tell, he lives alone. There's a small cut behind his ear that's already cemented brown with dried blood. Enoch estimates that he most likely cut himself while shaving earlier this morning. A lover, friend, companion, roommate—anyone—would have told him to address the small wound before leaving home.

In fact, it surprises Enoch terribly that a such an immaculately groomed gentleman might have lapsed in judgment and missed such an offensive detail. In the few moments Enoch can assess the small shopkeeper, he can tell his fastidiousness is matched only by his tenderness and care when putting himself together in the morning. Both of his patent leather loafers look as if they had been shined with the finest polish. In fact, they've been polished so vigorously that they chirp like starving baby birds when he first approaches Enoch. His moustache is coiffed so exaggeratedly and so impeccably that one might wonder if the thing were real in the first place.

Enoch can't quite place his finger on it, but there's something about him—something that worries him, deeply troubles him. For some reason, he can't seem to move past the small nick behind his ear. How could a man with such flawless care and precision when presenting himself allow something so apparently obscene go unnoticed? After all, as someone who had worked in sales for many years, Enoch knows full well that there's a very delicate art—a balancing act—when presenting yourself to the public scrutiny. For some reason, Enoch feels worried when he notices the fault in the shopkeeper's otherwise immaculate presentation—fearful he might see more, scared that there are other faults waiting to be confessed.

The store is one of those "blink-and-you'll-miss-it" type of places down near the waterfront—an old factory building now converted to various shops and restaurants to attract tourists. The shop is framed between two large entrances of two separate dining establishments—both outfitted with expensively decorated signage and even four fluted columns running up the length of the brick building wreathed with vines. If Enoch hadn't known precisely where to enter, he might have missed it. There are no signs, no details explaining what kind of service patrons may expect. He had only come to discover the shop's relatively new existence thanks to a painstaking internet search when he was hunting for places that sold various kinds of cutlery.

"Good afternoon, sir," the shopkeeper says, nearing Enoch with a look of sincerity—a regretful kind of look that belies some of the impishness residing in the corners of his eyes.

He looks as if he's genuinely sorry to disturb Enoch before he's had a moment to collect himself, but also somewhat eager for the possibility of conversation.

"Good afternoon," Enoch says, closing his umbrella and setting it down beside the coat rack arranged near the shop's small entryway. "Unseasonably chilly today, isn't it?"

Enoch expects him to force a half-hearted smile or concur with him about his insipid comment about the weather, but he doesn't. The shopkeeper seems to study him with the inquisitive eyes of a sculptor—meticulously calculating his design, his masterpiece, his creation. For a moment, Enoch feels unsettled. He feels as if he is somehow inadequately dressed, or as if he, himself, has allowed a small cut on his face to go overlooked.

"What brings you in today?" he asks Enoch, offering to

peel the raincoat from his arms as he shrugs it off. "You look as though you're here with purpose."

Although it had to have been fairly obvious that Enoch arrived with a certain level of urgency—a distinct level of hastiness that always seems to separate the window shoppers from the actual buyers—it makes Enoch wonder if the shopkeeper had spotted him while he was moving down the street. Something unsettles Enoch and whispers to him that the shopkeeper somehow knew he was planning on visiting today. He can't quite tell whether he admires that level of scrutiny from a store owner or whether it troubles him greatly. After all, salesmanship is all about anticipating the needs of others. Regardless, it unsettles Enoch to think that the shopkeeper might have expected him all along.

"I'm looking for a Santoku knife," Enoch says to him.

He notices the shopkeeper squint at him, visibly puzzled. Enoch senses his cheeks heat red, warmth flushing his face out of nervousness that he's somehow mispronounced the name.

Without hesitation, he digs deep into his pocket and pulls out a small notecard that his husband has prepared for him. In his exquisite cursive lettering, his husband has written "SANTOKU KNIFE" in capital letters simply because he knows full well that Enoch is far too vain to wear his prescribed eyewear in the middle of the afternoon.

"I think I pronounced it correctly," Enoch says to the shopkeeper. "It's a Japanese chef's knife, according to my husband."

The shopkeeper simpers, visibly amused. "For a moment,

I thought I had misheard you. We don't usually see many guests inquiring about such expensive cutlery."

"Are they expensive?" Enoch asks him, dreading the shopkeeper's answer. "My husband is particular, you see? We're expecting house guests this weekend and he wants to prepare a special meal for them."

The shopkeeper motions for Enoch to follow him toward a corner of the store where an arrangement of neatly polished glass cases meet.

"What kind of meat will you be serving?" he asks Enoch.

Enoch scrambles, referring to the note once more. Of course, his husband had told him; however, he neglected to include the name of the specific meat on the notecard he had prepared for him.

"I'm afraid I don't know," Enoch tells the shopkeeper. "He cooks more than I do, you see? He told me the meat was imported from the same village in France where he grew up. His parents' favorite butchery."

The shopkeeper's eyes narrow at Enoch. He already seems exasperated with the poor man's unskillfulness when it comes to cutlery. "The kind of meat is important. I could be more specific with my recommendations for knives if I knew exactly what you were serving."

Enoch senses himself curl inward, embarrassed. He curses himself, knowing full well that he should have had Cedric come to the store with him at the very least. It's not as if he wasn't able to come with Enoch. In fact, he had left him sleeping on the couch while an old black-and-white Greta Garbo movie played.

"For instance, a boning knife is perfect for cutting away the layer of fat on lamb prior to cooking," the shopkeeper explains. "But I seldom recommend the boning knife to customers if they're cooking filet mignon."

Enoch pockets the small notecard his husband had prepared for him, sensing more warmth heating both of his cheeks. "I'm—afraid I'm not as prepared as I thought I was."

For a moment, Enoch stands there and privately hopes the shopkeeper might say something to placate him, to rescue him from his awkwardness. Instead, the shopkeeper merely stares at him with a vacant expression that seems to confirm Enoch's humiliation.

"Perhaps I should come back another time," Enoch says, turning and beginning to move toward the coat rack to collect his raincoat.

"Nonsense," the shopkeeper says. "We can certainly try to pair you with the right cutlery for your lovely dinner party."

With a delicate sense of urgency that seems to hint at some of the more pressing aspects of the shopkeeper's desire to issue a sale today, the shopkeeper hooks Enoch's arm and drags him further into the store, until they're at another glass case that's filled with various neatly shined blades and other expensive-looking cutlery. The shopkeeper slides open the case and draws out a large knife with a gilded handle. Enoch senses himself tremor slightly. It's not that he's opposed to the outlandishness of the piece— well, *weapon* is probably the more appropriate term— but he can't help but imagine the high price for such a seemingly well-crafted and extravagant-looking knife. The shopkeeper holds the knife with both hands and lays it out on an embroidered cloth he's placed on top of the counter. He presents it to Enoch with the respect and dedication of a lowly serf presenting a sacred artifact to his master.

"What do you think of this gem?" the shopkeeper asks Enoch, eyeing him with a look of playfulness—a look that seems to say all at once, *Don't be shy. Tell me what you think.*

Enoch finds himself drawing closer and closer to the knife spread out on the glass counter, eager to touch it and yet also very much aware that his hands might insult the knife's beauty and magnificence.

"What do you call this one?" Enoch asks the shopkeeper, bending slightly and studying the large knife—from the small blood-like gemstones thatched in the knife's gold-plated handle to the terrifying sharpness of the blade.

"You are smitten with it?" the shopkeeper asks him.

Enoch exhales deeply, finally remembering to breathe. "It's—magnificent."

The shopkeeper pulls the knife closer toward him, as if noticing how Enoch has suddenly drawn so close that his breath is fogging the edge of the blade.

"You'll be mindful to be exceptionally careful with this one," the shopkeeper tells Enoch. "It's the option I typically suggest to most who are seeking a knife that will perform extraordinarily in the kitchen. After all, using a knife while cooking is like making love. The working equipment is important and usually makes for a better experience for all."

Enoch senses his cheeks heat with warmth again. Of course, he understands the shopkeeper's intention of saying something so decidedly vulgar, but it unsettles him all the same.

"I imagine something so... *marvelous* must be rather expensive, no?" Enoch asks, quietly fearing the shopkeeper's response.

"The price is always so important to you?" the shopkeeper responds.

Enoch recoils slightly at the bluntness of the shopkeeper's reply. Of course the price is important. The price would be critical for any uninformed shopper visiting the store, Enoch thinks to himself.

"The problem with most people is they think about what something will cost *them*," the shopkeeper says. "They don't consider what their purchase will offer them in return."

Enoch tilts his head at the shopkeeper, eyes narrowing to mere slits, struggling to comprehend.

"A purchase like this will change your life," the shopkeeper tells Enoch. "I expect more shoppers consider it a loss to their pocketbook when they buy something. But I always urge them to reconsider—to think of what they're *gaining*."

Enoch supposes that the shopkeeper is correct. After all, it seems all too inherent to think of buying something as losing a piece of one's wealth. But, for Enoch, he can't help but think of the majesty and grandeur this purchase will bring him. More to the point, there's something about the shopkeeper that mesmerizes him, transfixes him. He wants to impress him. He wants to connect with him in such a way that will make him stay in good graces with the charismatic shopkeeper.

"I suppose the price is unimportant," Enoch says. "The

knife is exceptional. You think it will be ideal for our dinner party?"

"I think it will—*transform* your life," the shopkeeper tells him. "I have no doubts."

Enoch slips his hand into his pocket and pulls out his leather wallet. "Will you wrap it up for me? I'd like to surprise my husband with it."

The shopkeeper nods, smiling. "Of course."

"And how much—?" Enoch asks the shopkeeper, sliding a credit card across the counter toward him.

Funnily enough, the shopkeeper waves the card away before he crosses his arms.

"How much is this knife worth to you?" the shopkeeper asks him.

Enoch stammers at first, perplexed. "I'm afraid I—don't understand."

"If you were to put a price on something as magnificent, as glorious as this knife, what would you say?" the shopkeeper asks. "More to the point, what would you do to acquire this knife?"

Enoch shakes his head, uncertain, and wonders if he heard the shopkeeper correctly. "What would I do—?"

The shopkeeper simpers, visibly amused. "I can see you're not as creative as I had hoped you might be."

Enoch's face scrunches, bewildered. "I'm afraid I don't know what—"

"I have a proposition for you," the shopkeeper tells Enoch, cutting him off. "I'll let you have the knife. I'll wrap it for you in beautiful tissue paper. I'll slip it inside a bag so you can surprise your husband with it. But I don't want money in exchange for the knife. I want you to do something for me."

Enoch senses all the color drain from his face. He can't help but imagine what horrible things the shopkeeper could have in mind as another form of payment. His mind immediately wanders to something obscene and sexual. Of course, there's something powerfully alluring about the shopkeeper—something devastatingly unique about him—but Enoch couldn't do something so vile behind his husband's back. That would be unforgiveable.

"Perhaps now isn't the best time," Enoch says, recoiling slightly from the shopkeeper and inching toward the door.

"All I ask is that you let me cut you," the shopkeeper says, his voice thinning to a whisper.

Enoch stops himself, wondering if the shopkeeper had truly just uttered something so unsettling.

"You want to—?"

"I want you to let me cut you with this knife," the shopkeeper tells him. "A very tiny cut. You'll hardly even feel it. I'll make certain that I'm as gentle as can be."

Enoch senses his stomach curling with unease.

"Then, when I'm finished, you'll let me insert a small piece of glass inside the cut," the shopkeeper tells him. "And that will be it."

Enoch shakes his head in disbelief. "You want to cut me open and stick a piece of glass inside—?"

The shopkeeper chuckles slightly at the crudeness of Enoch's assessment. "The way you say it doesn't make it sound as poetic as I had hoped. But yes. That's what I want from you. When finished, the knife will be yours and I'll send you on your way."

Enoch can hardly believe what the shopkeeper is suggesting. It seems too outlandish—too decidedly macabre—to take seriously. Still, there's a quiet part of Enoch that remains curious. He finds himself sincerely considering the shopkeeper's peculiar offer and his inquisitiveness frightens him. There's a curious and daring part of him that tells him it will be over before he knows it and he will then be on his way. Why should he turn down such a simple offer?

"You're certain it won't hurt?" Enoch asks the shopkeeper.

"I'll make sure of it."

Enoch thinks again. He's surprised with himself, astonished that he's so seriously considering the shopkeeper's unusual offer. There's something about the offer that excites a part of him that has been undisturbed for so long—a part of him that's now newly awakening and stretching itself free.

"Very well," Enoch says.

The shopkeeper says nothing. He merely smiles.

After the shopkeeper tells Enoch to roll up his shirt sleeve to expose his right arm, the shopkeeper swipes the knife from the countertop and prepares for his labor. Enoch watches in silence as the shopkeeper studies his exposed arm, visibly outlining where he'll choose to mark his skin for incision. Enoch says nothing when the shopkeeper presses the ice-cold tip of the blade against his arm, lingering there for a moment before eventually slicing down and opening the tiny, angry mouth of a wound in his naked skin. Enoch glances down and notices a line of dark red creeping from the hole the shopkeeper has opened there. The shopkeeper snatches a nearby cloth and presses it against the small wound until some of the bleeding stops.

The shopkeeper orders Enoch to keep the cloth pressed against the tiny wound for a moment while he circles the counter and disappears into the back room. As Enoch stands there, cloth pressed against the leaking wound, he wonders why he agreed to something so unusual. Had he merely wanted to remain in good graces with the shopkeeper? Why should he care what the shopkeeper thought of him? Or was he excited by the notion of something so unusual, something so decidedly peculiar? As Enoch thinks, he comes to the realization that perhaps he likes the uncertainty of the situation. After all, his life has been so neatly ordered that it is refreshing to partake in something that seems to have no rhyme or reason.

The shopkeeper finally returns with a small velvet bag with a drawstring. He pulls the drawstring and tilts the bag open on the counter. Small, glittering specks of glass spill out from inside the bag and scatter across the table like a tide of hail. The shopkeeper seizes a pair of tweezers and pinches a speck of glass there. Then he approaches Enoch with the same intent he possessed when he first approached him with the large knife.

"This may hurt a little," the shopkeeper tells him. "I promise I won't go too deep."

Enoch winces slightly, glancing away, as he senses the shopkeeper push the tiny piece of glass between his wound's puckered lips. Stirring there for a moment, the shopkeeper finally draws the tweezers out from inside Enoch, and he marvels at his handiwork. Enoch flinches slightly when the shopkeeper touches his skin, squeezing the edges of the wound together as if forcing them to close over the broken bit of glass he's slid inside.

"You'll have to take the glass out later tonight," the shopkeeper tells Enoch. "Otherwise, it'll become infected. You have tweezers at home?"

Enoch can't answer at first. He can't even seem to think of home and where he'll eventually be headed. None of that seems to matter right now. He feels lost, unmoored, and adrift as if he were swept out to sea during a rainstorm. He's surprised when he senses how much he revels in the exquisiteness of the uncertainty, the marvelousness of the absurdity.

"Yes," he finally replies to the shopkeeper. "We have tweezers."

Without hesitation, the shopkeeper returns to the counter and begins to carefully wrap the large knife. Then, when he's finished wrapping the item, he cranes his head beneath the counter and pulls out a small black bag with the store's logo emblazoned on the front. He slips the wrapped knife inside and then passes the bag to Enoch, their hands touching slightly.

"I hope you and your husband have a lovely dinner party," the shopkeeper says to him. "You certainly have the correct equipment now."

Enoch thinks to say something, but all words seem

impossible. He merely takes the bag from the shopkeeper and then ambles toward the coat rack where he's set his coat and umbrella. After slipping on his coat, he glances back at the shopkeeper and notices himself regarding him the way a lover might observe their one true love before a final farewell. He finds it odd that he thinks of the shopkeeper in such a way. Of course, he's still enchanted by him, but why should he think of him so fondly?

The shopkeeper waves at him, and finally Enoch twists the handle and passes out through the shop's front entrance. As he meanders down the street, rain pattering the top of his umbrella, Enoch senses the small broken bit of glass stirring inside the tiny wound in his arm. For once in his life, Enoch is filled with a strange kind of excitement—an excitement that seems to beg him to consider all the other opportunities he had neglected, a delight that implores him to open more of his skin and fill himself with things he had never considered before.

TWO

When Enoch finally returns home after taking the long way back to the apartment, he finds his husband, Cedric, milling about in the kitchen and chopping up hazelnuts for a fresh salad. For some inexplicable reason, the sight of his husband nearly makes him retch. He can't help but wonder why. After all, he has never regarded Cedric that way before. He has always observed his beloved husband with such sympathy and uncompromising tenderness. Why should today be so different? He's reminded, of course, when he flexes his arm and senses the little broken bit of glass stirring inside the small wound.

"You were gone for quite some time," Cedric says to Enoch, glancing at him as he continues chopping the hazelnuts littered about the cutting board. "Good shopping trip I imagine?"

Enoch thinks to say something but can't for some reason. All words seem hollow and inconsequential. Instead, he replies by setting the black bag on the counter and pulling out the wrapped knife. He passes the item to Cedric with a forced smile.

"It feels heavy," Cedric says, eyes widening as he begins to unwrap the item. "That must mean it was expensive."

Enoch swallows hard. "Not as much as you might think."

"How much?" Cedric asks.

Enoch senses himself pale, uncertain how to reply at first.

"Go on," he orders his husband. "I want to see your reaction."

Finally, Cedric peels the wrapping paper off and reveals the gilded handle thatched with bits of jewelry and the impressively shined blade. He covets the weapon, cradling it as if it were a precious newborn.

"My God," he says, blinking in disbelief. "It's... *beautiful.*"

Enoch relaxes a little, letting his guard down bit by bit. "The shopkeeper said it would be perfect for us. I told him all about our upcoming dinner party and what we needed."

Cedric finally pulls his eyes away from the impressive blade and stares Enoch down. "How much was it—?"

Enoch clears the catch in his throat, squeezing his arm until he flinches in agony as if it were a penance for his treachery, his deceitfulness.

"Are you happy with it?" Enoch asks his husband. "I hope you are."

Cedric regards the knife again, his eyes going over and over the blade once more. "It's... *perfect.*"

Without warning, Cedric pulls Enoch tight against him and presses his lips against his. Enoch winces slightly, hiding his discomfort as best he can, when Cedric squeezes the side of his arm while he embraces him. Enoch senses the little broken bit of glass slipping deeper and deeper inside the sleeve of exposed tissue that the shopkeeper had opened in his skin. He wonders if he'll ever be able to reach it with a pair of tweezers now. Perhaps he won't. Perhaps the damned thing will live inside him until his wound finally closes and his body claims it as its own. Enoch doesn't mind thinking of that scenario. In fact, he's surprised when he finds it pleases him to think about.

"Will you pour me a glass of wine?" Enoch asks Cedric. "I just have to clean up before dinner."

Cedric pecks him on the cheek before Enoch slips out of the kitchen and into the bedroom. He skirts into the bathroom and rolls up his sleeve to reveal the tiny wound once more. He angles his arm in such a way that he can inspect it further in the mirror. He's surprised how the rusted brown lips of the wound have already seemed to come together, threatening to close forever. Swiping a pair of tweezers from the medicine cabinet, Enoch pushes the tip inside the small wound and roots around for the shard of glass. Finally capturing it, he pulls it until the broken bit of glass arrives in the light. He stares at the sliver for a moment—inspecting the sharpness of its edges, admiring the beads of blood webbing on it.

I can't bear to part with this, he thinks to himself. *Not yet.*

He's alarmed to admit it, but there's a part of him that secretly enjoys knowing the bit of glass is deep inside him, courting his insides and wooing his blood to flow freely.

With one swift motion that decides the matter instantly, Enoch pushes the small bit of glass back inside the wound until it disappears completely and the lips close shut like the entrance of a tomb. He shudders slightly. He's fearful to confess, but he finds himself becoming especially excited—yes, perhaps even aroused—as he senses the shard of glass working its way deeper and deeper inside his arm. Before becoming too enraptured in his ecstasy, he adjusts himself where his legs meet and makes his way out of the bathroom and into the kitchen.

Cedric pulls a tray of roasted chicken from the oven and sets the platter on the stovetop. Enoch notices a glass of red wine waiting for him on the edge of the kitchen counter.

"Mine?" he asks his husband.

"Enjoy," Cedric tells him.

Without hesitation, Enoch reaches out to swipe the glass of wine from the counter, but instead he knocks the glass from the edge and sends it shattering against the tiled kitchen floor. Cedric leaps, startled at the noise.

"Shit," Enoch says, regarding the remnants of the wine glass scattered about the floor and the wine as dark as blood curling across the tiles.

"Don't worry," Cedric tells him. "I'll get the broom and bucket."

When Cedric disappears into the nearby pantry, Enoch finds himself compelled to step down on the broken bits of glass littered about the floor. He wonders what it might feel like—the tiny shards gluing to his skin and poking deep inside until they vanish. He's just about to do it when Cedric returns and starts sweeping the shattered bits into a bucket. Enoch watches in hate-filled silence as the glass shards are pulled away from him and dumped into the trash can. While he observes, he can't help but think to himself: *What a waste. What a truly and utterly dreadful waste.*

After a mostly sleepless night, Enoch wakes late in the morning and finds Cedric's side of the bed already dressed and covered. He stirs, listening to the sound of his husband beyond the closed bathroom door, humming while he lathers his face with shaving cream. Cringing slightly, Enoch thinks of the dreams he had endured last night—dreams of long, needle-thin spindles of painted glass sprouting from beneath the tips of his fingernails and fanning out in their monstrous glory. He thinks of how he dreamt of thin stems of more cathedral-like painted glass furrowing the skin on his backside and unfurling in regal splendor as if he were a frightening creature from a children's storybook.

Enoch is quick to recognize that the dreams hadn't unsettled him the way they once might have. Instead, they had inspired him, moved him—yes, perhaps even noticeably aroused him. He finds himself growing stiff between his legs and pushes himself down until he's no longer poking out so obscenely from beneath his underwear.

Before straightening out of bed, Enoch pushes his hand against the small wound in his arm—the edges of the wound now crusted black and difficult to pry open without causing immeasurable agony. He pushes the tip of his pinky finger inside the small opening and senses the jagged edge of the splinter of glass deep inside—right where he had left it. His eyes drift from the wound to the small glass of water arranged on the nightstand.

He thinks of Cedric and how kind his husband is to always set a glass of water beside him in case he needs a drink in the middle of the night. Enoch trembles, imagining how it might feel to smash the glass on the edge of the nightstand and then drive one of the glass splinters into his stomach— sliding the shattered bit so deep inside that his intestines spill out like garlands at Christmastime.

His eyes remain fixed on the small glass of water. He thinks of picking it up and slamming it down so that it cracks, so that a tiny piece breaks off—something else he could take to stuff inside the small opening the shopkeeper had already so kindly and meticulously wrinkled in his arm. Just as Enoch is about to swipe the glass from the nightstand, Cedric appears in the bathroom doorway.

"I have to go into the office today," he explains. "A client from Chicago is flying in for a two o'clock meeting."

Enoch withdraws a little, eyes avoiding the glass of water at all costs.

"Will you be staying late tonight?" he asks.

"I might get corralled into taking him out for dinner with his wife," Cedric says. "You're welcome to join if you'd like?"

Enoch, of course, loathes the idea. There's nothing he'd like less than to spend the evening with a boring pair of out-of-town dolts and pretend to be interested in what they have to say.

Before Enoch can respond, Cedric slips back into the

bathroom and resumes shaving at the mirror. Part of Enoch wonders if Cedric truly and sincerely meant to invite him to dinner with his guests. Not that he wanted to attend anyway. Still, there's a distrustful part of him that wonders if Cedric detests bringing him to his work commitments because of his homophobic colleagues.

"Oh, I almost forgot to tell you," Cedric says, poking his head out from the bathroom doorway. "That knife you brought home yesterday is a piece of junk."

Enoch recoils slightly, wondering if he heard his husband correctly.

"Piece of junk?" Enoch asks. "You—said it was marvelous."

"I thought it was," Cedric says, rolling his eyes. "Until one of the red gemstones fell out from its setting in the handle."

Enoch swallows nervously. "One of the gems fell out—?"

"Go to the kitchen and see for yourself," Cedric says to him, returning to the mirror and gliding a razor up the length of his throat. "I left it on the counter."

Enoch flies from the bedroom and into the kitchen. He comes upon the knife lying on the cutting board on the counter, immediately noticing how one of the gemstones is missing from the handle. Enoch glances around, noticing the tiny red bead has rolled underneath a nearby dish. He scoops it up and collects it in his palm. Then he pockets it.

For a moment, Enoch thinks of searching for the shop's telephone number online and giving the shopkeeper a call to complain about the defective product. But as he considers this, he entertains a more appealing option—to return to the small store and see the shopkeeper again.

The thought excites him terribly. In fact, he senses the crotch of his pants shortening when imagining all the possibilities that could transpire between him and the shopkeeper if they were left unchaperoned once more. After all, Enoch had invented scenario after scenario in his mind of what the shopkeeper could offer to him, what the shopkeeper could do to him. Each scenario— each one cruder and more obscene than the last—excites Enoch to the point where he wonders if he'll ever want to return home. Although he despises to admit it, his time at home with Cedric has felt different ever since he met the shopkeeper. Of course, he knows full well how tenderly and prudently Cedric cares for him and loves him. Regardless, there's a part of Enoch desperate for the same thrill he had felt yesterday when in the shopkeeper's presence—when the shopkeeper had cut him open and pushed the broken bit of glass inside him.

It isn't long before Cedric arrives in the kitchen fully dressed in his suit for work. He pecks Enoch on the cheek with a kiss and then begins to pour himself coffee in a to-go cup.

"I told you it broke," Cedric says, swiping an apple from the kitchen counter and pocketing it for later. "It's junk."

"I'll head back to the shop today and ask for a refund," Enoch tells him. "That's ridiculous. It's supposed to be of the highest quality. He said it was, at least."

"Be careful that con artist of a store owner doesn't try to sell you anything else," Cedric warns him. "They're tricky like that."

Enoch smiles politely.

Cedric grabs his coat from the rack beside the door, then kisses his husband once more before slipping out of the apartment and ambling down the hall with his briefcase in hand. After Enoch watches his husband drift away and out of sight, he closes the apartment door and returns to the kitchen counter. There, he comes upon the knife once more. Although he's disappointed with the knife's inferior craftsmanship, he's grateful for it as well. After all, how else might he have invented an excuse to return to the store to visit the shopkeeper?

Enoch makes no delay. He hurries into the bathroom and strips naked before leaping into the shower stall. He washes himself, careful to not disturb the wound or to somehow wrench the small bit of glass from inside. His fingers, ever curious, begin to tease the tiny opening while he scrubs himself. He senses himself hardening until he's fully erect. Then, while merely poking his finger inside the small wound and rummaging about, he brings himself to a violent orgasm. It's the first time in months he's done so, and it pains him a little bit—a current of anguish squeezing his manhood and holding him there until the last of it dribbles out from him and down the drain.

For the first time, he hadn't thought of Cedric while pleasuring himself as was his usual custom. In fact, he hadn't thought of the beguiling shopkeeper either. He's surprised to admit to himself that he had thought of recovering more broken bits of glass and inventing new wounds on his body where they could permanently live. Still, there's something ever so alluring about the shopkeeper and his prowess when it comes to self-mutilation. Of course, Enoch could do the gruesome deed while Cedric was away at work for the day; however, there's something more exciting about venturing back to the store and entertaining the prospect of his body absorbing another shard of glass.

After he finishes scrubbing himself and getting dressed, Enoch shoves the knife into the black bag and heads out of the apartment. He thinks of meandering through the nearby park on his way to the shop as he had done yesterday.

Not today, he thinks to himself.

There's a distinct urgency compelling him today and he'd be damned if he allowed an opportunity to bask in the shopkeeper's presence to go to waste. Enoch's heart races as he hurries to the shop and, for a moment, he wonders if he's flying. The wound in his arm begins to ache, but that's very little price to pay for such rapture, such indescribable ecstasy.

THREE

Enoch bristles coolly as he makes his way toward the storefront. As soon as his eyes come upon the store's entrance, he senses his pace slow to a crawl. He wonders if he should step inside. Of course, he had intended to visit the shopkeeper to return the defective knife; however, his intentions were hardly as benign and as simple as that. The shopkeeper had aroused him, the shopkeeper had awakened bewildering feelings within him that had been dormant since he had married Cedric.

Enoch thinks of turning away, of pocketing the knife and merely accepting the loss. It's then that the side of his arm pains him, the broken bit of glass shifting further and further inside him. He certainly can't ignore that, no matter how unremittingly he tried. He could never forget the sensations, the ecstasies he had felt when the shopkeeper had first pushed the shard of glass inside his open wound.

Although it is foolish to consider, Enoch sincerely

wonders if he might come apart—if he might totally unravel and come undone—if the bit of glass were taken from his open wound. Enoch feels as if the splintered bit of glass were now a permanent part of him, like an organ. He'd be damned before he allowed anyone to take it away from him. Moreover, he can't help but entertain the thought of other bits of glass from the shopkeeper and how they might feel inside him.

In one swift motion that decides the matter instantly, Enoch pulls on the door handle and thrusts himself into the shop. He glances around the small room and his eyes finally come upon what he's been searching for—the shopkeeper, framed in the corner of the room where the walls meet, squatting on a stool and polishing the blade of a large knife. Although Enoch has rehearsed his speech time and time again while journeying to the store, all words flee from his mind and momentarily he's left without reason for his visit. The shopkeeper rises from his seat and begins to approach him. Enoch guards himself with the small black bag as if it were his only protection.

"You came back to tell me just how much your husband loved the knife?" the shopkeeper says, laughing heartily. "I had a feeling he would."

Enoch collects himself quietly. "Not quite," he says. "I'm afraid there's a problem with the item you sold me."

Enoch sets the bag on the counter and pulls out the knife, brandishing it in front of the shopkeeper for him to see. Enoch tilts the knife into the light so the shopkeeper can see the missing gemstone insulting the weapon's handle.

"One of the gemstones fell out, you see?"

The shopkeeper leans over the counter, eyes squinting as he inspects the knife. He draws in so close that Enoch feels the warmth of his breath gently heating his skin.

"So it did," the shopkeeper says. "How… unusual."

"Normally, I wouldn't complain," Enoch says, feeling a bit foolish for his criticism in the first place. "But my husband noticed the missing gem and was rather upset. He wants everything at this dinner party to be as perfect as possible."

"Naturally," the shopkeeper tells him.

There's a long beat of silence between the two of them—an uncomfortable silence that lingers over the room like the presence of an unwelcome guest. Enoch wonders if the shopkeeper will offer to make the situation right. He hopes he will, at the very least. But, instead, the shopkeeper simply glares at Enoch with seemingly no intention of saying anything to comfort him.

"I—don't suppose you have another knife to replace this one," Enoch says eventually, his voice trembling a little.

The shopkeeper's eyes narrow at Enoch. A smile worms its way across his face.

"That's not the reason you came here," the shopkeeper says to him.

Enoch senses his cheeks heat red as if he has been caught. Of course, he had intended to return the knife. But the shopkeeper is correct. Enoch had returned to the store to seek out other opportunities, other sensations that weren't possible with Cedric. Is he so disgusting for considering something so vile? Enoch isn't certain.

He straightens, collecting his composure. "I—don't know what you mean."

"If I may ask: how's your arm?" the shopkeeper asks him.

Enoch winces. "Pains me a little."

"Let me see it."

Without hesitation, the shopkeeper grabs hold of Enoch's arm and rolls up his sleeve to expose the wound he had opened there yesterday. The shopkeeper grins with such unreserved delight as his eyes covet the small wound—the flexing lips crusted black with dried blood.

"You've been playing with it, haven't you—?"

Enoch stammers, too embarrassed to answer without lying.

The shopkeeper suddenly notices something. He draws in closer toward the wound, prying the lips open a little bit and peeking inside. He exhales deeply.

"You left the broken bit of glass inside—?"

Enoch doesn't quite know how to respond. He could leave if he had a mind to. He could swipe the knife from the counter and fly out the door, never to return. Or he could simply tell the shopkeeper the truth.

"I—like the way it feels," he says softly, clutching his arm a little tighter as if holding the glass shard in place. "I didn't think I would, but I like knowing it's there—knowing it's inside me."

The shopkeeper's eyes are listless, vacant. "You've thought of adding more bits of glass, haven't you—?"

Enoch's eyes lower, unsure how to answer at first.

I might as well tell him the truth, he thinks.

"Yes," he says. "It feels… remarkable."

The shopkeeper smiles warmly. "I thought you might say that."

Without warning, the shopkeeper lifts his shirt and exposes his hairless stomach—the skin pockmarked with crusted wounds, a shiny bit of glass poking out from the entrance of each wound. Enoch's eyes don't know where to search first. He draws in close, examining the tiny openings yawning back at him from the shopkeeper's exposed stomach. Just as he's about to reach out and touch the edge of a shard of glass, the shopkeeper pulls away from him.

Enoch apologizes with a look. Then he collects himself.

"What about—infection?" he asks the shopkeeper.

"I'm careful to remove each bit of glass every night," the shopkeeper explains. "I put them back in place in the morning."

Enoch's mind begins to race. There are millions of questions screaming at him in the privacy of his mind. But what to ask first?

"You've been doing this for long?" Enoch asks him.

"Long enough to know how to make the most out of it," the shopkeeper says.

Enoch's mind continues to race. Just then, as the shopkeeper turns his head slightly, Enoch notices the small cut behind the shopkeeper's ear he had first seen yesterday. What he hadn't seen was a transparent sliver of glass poking out from the small wound. How could he have missed that before?

"Are there ways to hide it—?" Enoch asks him.

"Seems like you're already quite skilled at that," the shopkeeper says, visibly amused. "I gather your husband wouldn't be pleased—?"

Enoch merely shakes his head. His tone firms. "I—don't want him to ever find out."

"There are ways for you to enjoy yourself—to live authentically—without compromising your marriage," the shopkeeper says to Enoch, his hand crawling across the counter and reaching for Enoch's.

Just as their hands come together, the shop's main entrance is flung open and a group of various men and women file inside the store. They're all well dressed and groomed immaculately. The ladies remove their expensive-looking hats while the gentlemen shrug off their coats and hang them from the nearby coat rack. They seem to move about the shop as if very comfortable, as if they surely and truly belong here and have always belonged here. They do not resemble the passive and quite often fatigued window shoppers typically looking to waste away a Friday afternoon. Instead, they command the space with a purpose that immediately intimidates Enoch.

He senses himself recoil slightly, as he does normally around large groups of people. He's especially unnerved when the group of ladies and gentlemen approach and pass him as they make their way toward the door leading to the back room. The shopkeeper waves at them as they pass.

"Perhaps I should go," Enoch says, shoving the knife into the black bag and threatening to tear himself away in a matter of seconds. "I don't want to keep you."

"Nonsense," the shopkeeper says, circling in front of

the counter and making his way toward the shop's main entrance. "You're in time for our meeting. I imagine you'll want to stay for this."

"Meeting—?" Enoch asks him, hands nervously fumbling together.

"A small group of my friends," the shopkeeper replies. "Enthusiasts of a similar nature."

Enoch struggles to comprehend. "They also—?"

The shopkeeper fastens the lock on the store entrance and posts a sign in the window that reads: *Gone to lunch. Will return in one hour.*

When he has finished drawing the curtains over the few windows overlooking the street outside, the shopkeeper makes his way toward Enoch once more.

"I think you should stay," the shopkeeper tells Enoch. "You'll be glad you did."

Before Enoch can respond, the shopkeeper slips away from him and meanders over to the door leading to the back room. He glances at Enoch one final time and then disappears inside. Enoch feels his insides splitting apart as if he were made of damp straw. He knows full well once he crosses over the threshold, there is no turning back. There are no opportunities to end what he's started once the dance has finally begun. A sharp pang of agony coils its way up his arm—a sudden reminder that tells him in no uncertain terms that the dance has already started.

Realizing there's no point in denying he's already been issued a clear invitation, Enoch swallows hard and makes his way toward the door leading to the back room. While he stands at the threshold, he can't help but wonder what sights, what sensations the shopkeeper and his constituents will show him. Enoch knows full well there's only one way to find out.

———

As Enoch files inside the small room at the rear of the store, he notices how all the well-dressed attendees shift and regard him with such scrupulous curiosity. He recoils a little, feeling very much out of place. He feels particularly underdressed in his stained khakis and knitted sweater, seeing as the other gentlemen are wearing lavish, custom-tailored suits, while the women are gowned in equally impressive garments. As he inhales and exhales, he notices how most of the guests seem to accept his presence and glance away from him. Finally, he's not the center of attention.

Enoch inches further into the room, where the guests have assembled in chairs arranged in a large circle. He notices the shopkeeper loiter on the periphery for a moment and then drift into the middle of the enclosure, gesturing for Enoch to take an empty seat near where he's standing. Enoch obeys without comment, sitting beside an elderly gentleman with a beard and a middle-aged woman wearing the most ostentatious brooch of a golden dragonfly pinned to her collar.

Enoch watches silently as the shopkeeper mills in the center of the space, presumably waiting for the room to quiet before he speaks. When the chatter dims to a mere murmur, the shopkeeper addresses his guests and welcomes them with a polite grin.

"Friends," he says. "Today we are gathered to welcome a visitor."

Enoch senses his face pale, his stomach gurgling with indigestion. He hopes the shopkeeper isn't referring to him. His hopes are dashed immediately once the shopkeeper eyes him and asks him to stand and introduce himself. Although he wonders why he's being so obedient in the shopkeeper's presence, his indecision isn't enough to prevent him from submitting to the shopkeeper's each and every whim. Enoch rises from his seat and addresses the unimpressed throng of guests.

"Hi," he says shakily. "I'm Enoch."

He looks at the shopkeeper, as if begging to be rescued. He stammers, uncertain.

"I'm always terrible at these things," he confesses. "I suppose—I'm just very curious and looking to seek out new and exciting opportunities."

The shopkeeper nods. "You've certainly come to the right place, Enoch."

Whispers filter throughout the small crowd of guests, as if harmonizing with the shopkeeper.

"Blessed be those who come here," the shopkeeper says, closing his eyes and closing his hands together. "They will know salvation unlike anything else."

Enoch watches as the guests bow their heads, their lips moving with muted prayers. After they pray, the shopkeeper drifts to a table arranged in the corner of the room that's been decorated with various religious-looking paraphernalia. Enoch notices candles, books, matchsticks, and some crosses.

It isn't long before the shopkeeper returns, carrying a small velvet satchel that's bulging with something inside.

Enoch watches, mouth hanging open, as the crowd of guests begin to remove pieces of their clothing. Some gentlemen roll up their sleeves to reveal skin pocked with various cuts and bruises. Others unbutton shirts to expose their chests cratered with similar wounds. Some of the ladies remove their stockings and show the skin of their legs pitted with obscene bruising. Enoch looks closely and suddenly notices how there's a tiny shard of glass poking out from each and every open wound.

One by one, the shopkeeper goes to each guest and inserts a sliver of glass inside a fresh wound they had apparently opened earlier today. Enoch watches, stunned, while some of the guests convulse violently when the shopkeeper pushes the bit of glass inside them. Some of them thrash. Others clench their thighs together and squeeze tight, as if they were on the brink of an unbearable orgasm.

Finally, the shopkeeper arrives at Enoch. Although Enoch had prepared for this and had expected this, he goes wanting. The shopkeeper merely shakes his head at him and moves to the next guest in line. Enoch glances around the room, as if to appraise whether or not anyone was paying attention to his humiliation. Thankfully, most of the others are far too enraptured with the new bit of glass they've received from the shopkeeper or are touching themselves underneath their clothing.

When all have met with the shopkeeper, the guests begin to filter out through the door and back into the shop.

Enoch throws a look at the shopkeeper, hoping he might say something to him. But he doesn't. Instead, the shopkeeper makes a dash toward the main entrance, where he unlocks the door. The guests collect their coats and belongings before eventually meandering out through the shop's main entryway and into the bustling street.

Enoch composes himself, wondering what he could possibly say to the shopkeeper. After all, he had been invited to the meeting. But to be humiliated in front of everyone and denied what he so dreadfully desired seems almost too cruel to consider. Enoch wonders if this was all a ruse orchestrated by the shopkeeper. He wonders if the shopkeeper had simply invited him to attend just to disgrace him, to tease him with what would never be completely and utterly his.

Enoch doesn't seem to notice the shopkeeper approaching him until it's too late and he's already at his side.

"You're upset, I gather," the shopkeeper says to Enoch.

Enoch stammers, unsure how to answer.

"I invited you to our gathering so you could see what your life could become," the shopkeeper explains. "But I'm afraid you're far from being welcomed to the club."

Enoch swallows, bewildered. "It's a... club?"

"A coterie of enthusiasts," the shopkeeper says. "Whatever you want to call it. We meet daily and revel in our brief time together."

Enoch senses a pinch in the pit of his throat, cautious to ask. "How do you get them to trust you? How do you get invited in?"

"You've already been given a taste," the shopkeeper says. "You seem to like it. Otherwise, you wouldn't have returned. Now it's time for you to prove yourself."

Enoch recoils slightly, unnerved. "Prove what—?"

"Your dedication to the Order," the shopkeeper explains. "Surely, you don't expect us to believe you're truly and sincerely committed to our growth, our success, without actually proving yourself."

Enoch thinks for a moment. Of course, the shopkeeper makes some sense. Enoch doesn't necessarily expect the members of this private club to accept him with graciousness all at once. He recognizes fully that sometimes in life one must put one's comfort aside in order to prove one's integrity.

"I suppose you're right," Enoch says. "What will you have me do?"

"Every fledgling—every newcomer to our group—begins the same way," the shopkeeper says. "We assign them with the task of recruiting someone else, introducing another person to our fixation."

Enoch shakes his head in disbelief, uncertain what to say at first.

"You want me to find someone off the street?" Enoch asks, laughing.

The shopkeeper isn't as amused. He glares at Enoch, a little visibly suspicious for the first time. "How else will our group thrive? Without fresh blood? Without new skin to poke with bits of glass?"

Enoch hesitates. "You want me to recruit a random stranger—?"

"What were you exactly before I met you?" the shopkeeper asks him. "You were a stranger to me, weren't you?"

Enoch wonders. Of course, the shopkeeper is correct. They were strangers when they first met, and there's still so much of the shopkeeper that Enoch doesn't understand. However, there had been so many times—so many quiet moments—when Enoch wondered to himself if he had known the shopkeeper before. There was something about the shopkeeper—something so unusual and yet comforting— that made Enoch wonder if they had known one another in a former life.

"I—suppose strangers connect over unusual things all the time, don't they?" Enoch asks, hoping for a semblance of reassurance from the shopkeeper.

He merely nods.

"When do you want this new recruit?" Enoch asks him.

"Our next gathering is tomorrow at two in the afternoon," the shopkeeper says.

Enoch's stomach drops. "Tomorrow's our dinner party. We've been planning it for months."

The shopkeeper merely glares at Enoch. "The sooner you bring a new recruit, the sooner you'll be welcomed. You want that, don't you—?"

Of course, Enoch thinks to himself.

He wants that more than anything. After all, it's been nearly unbearable to exist in the shopkeeper's presence without being stabbed with a small shard of glass. Enoch shakes his head in disbelief, positively uncertain how he could have developed such an unusual and repulsive fetish.

Still, it's something that seems to define his life entirely. He reasons that he will now refer to his life in the span of two separate eras—"*Before Glass*" and "*After Glass*."

"Yes," Enoch replies. "I want that. More than anything."

The shopkeeper smiles in such a way that lets Enoch know he's pleased with him.

"Then I urge you to get to work," the shopkeeper says, passing Enoch a small velvet bag filled with broken bits of glass. "I expect to see you and our new recruit tomorrow afternoon."

The shopkeeper ushers Enoch toward the store's entryway and, without another word, pushes him out into the street. Enoch stumbles onto the sidewalk, a little dazed, and catches his footing. After collecting himself for a moment, he begins his journey back to the apartment. He winces each time he passes a stranger and doesn't introduce himself— all the missed opportunities of human connection, all the fulfillments gone to waste.

FOUR

While he makes his way home, Enoch's mind returns to the shopkeeper over and over again—from the meticulous presentation of the gentleman's well-coiffed moustache to the way his lips seem to purse whenever Enoch draws near. Enoch finds the thoughts nearly unbearable. Perhaps even more excruciating—the thought of recruiting a random stranger to the shopkeeper's unusual coterie. Of course, Enoch has never shied away from meeting new people and forging new relationships; however, how could he possibly convince someone to be attracted to something so grotesque, so obscene?

After all, it's such an unusual and decidedly peculiar fixation. Enoch hadn't realized that he cared for it until it had finally happened to him. He supposes he might get lucky and locate someone with a generously open mind. That said, it's also just as likely that he'll capture the attention of the wrong individual and consequently out the shopkeeper's private club to the whole community.

Finally, after a long walk, Enoch arrives home and finds the apartment empty. Naturally, he hadn't expected Cedric to have returned home before him. Still, he's unsettled when he realizes he's very much alone and will continue to be alone for the next few hours. It's not that he despises the thought of being on his own. Not at all. But, for some reason, it's almost intolerable for him to exist in an empty apartment right now. He thinks of heading back out onto the street and striking up a conversation with the first person he bumps into. He finds himself leaning toward the door, hands fumbling with the handle. But something suddenly stops him—something deep within that paralyzes him.

There's a part of Enoch that's afraid—fearful that he might come across someone who judges him for his predilection or, perhaps even worse, someone who's so enraptured with it that they lose their selves in one another. Of course, he doesn't want that to happen. Enoch knows full well how he loves Cedric and wants to go on loving him. In fact, he even wonders if he might be able to get away with bringing Cedric to the meeting tomorrow as a new recruit. But he shakes the thought away as soon as it comes, knowing full well that such an arrangement would never work for too many reasons to list.

Although a thought of the excitement and the rush of recruiting a new member fills his mind, it eventually dissipates like a low-hanging curtain of fog curling back out to sea. He sits in one of the living room chairs, holding the knife in his right hand and going over the gilded handle again and again. He does this for a few hours until Cedric finally arrives home. Enoch hides the defective knife where he knows Cedric will never look. Cedric asks Enoch if he's already eaten dinner. Enoch lies and tells his husband that he has, doing his best to quiet his gurgling stomach—the hunger that's been swelling within him for quite some time. They go to bed together, and it isn't until the following morning that Enoch tells Cedric he'll be going out for most of the day.

"The whole day?" Cedric asks him, hoisting a pair of jeans around his waist. "You remember the dinner party's tonight, don't you—?"

Enoch senses himself blush. "Yes. Of course. I won't be too long, I promise. I just have a few errands to take care of."

"Nothing that can wait—?" Cedric asks.

Enoch loathes how inquisitive Cedric has become so abruptly. He's never usually so investigative. But Enoch supposes that tonight's dinner party might be the reason for his husband's meddling curiosity.

After Enoch finishes washing himself and dressing, he swipes the black bag containing the knife from his hiding spot and makes his way out of the apartment. He calls to his husband, who's still getting dressed in the adjoining room, that he'll return later. Cedric agrees, his tone a little bristly. But Enoch suspects his husband will cool down and collect himself in a matter of hours once he's home again for the party.

Enoch eventually finds himself strolling through the large colonnade, taking in the open gallery of the public park as he passes across the narrow walkway. He tips his hat at others when they pass, and usually he's met with cordial hellos and other pleasant greetings. However, each person he passes doesn't seem to possess the qualities he's searching for in a new recruit. If asked to list those qualities, Enoch would blush and stammer with cloying uncertainty. He couldn't possibly name the qualities he was searching for or the type of person he needed to find. He simply knew that when the person appeared to him, he would know full well that they were the perfect match for him.

After circling the large pond flanked by various hedges and other bits of greenery, Enoch meanders toward a small bench positioned on the side of a pathway leading to the park's main gate. He figures he'll be able to clearly see all who enter and leave. Moreover, he reasons, with such a prime location, he'll be able to make the most of his assessment and take his time when slimming down his choices. After all, since it's such a busy afternoon in the park, he's optimistic he'll be able to commandeer someone within an hour or so.

As he perches on the bench, he sets the black bag between his feet. Occasionally, he glances down and spots the knife and the small satchel filled with broken bits of glass the shopkeeper had given him. His eyes wander to the nearby hillside, where he sees children racing one another from one end of the park to the other. He notices young men and women, their arms intertwined, strolling up and down the pathway in front of where he's seated.

That won't do, he thinks to himself.

Enoch knows full well he needs to find someone who's

noticeably isolated—someone who hasn't arrived at the park with a companion. He continues his search, his attention becoming weaker and weaker as the minutes pass. Enoch thinks of slipping away to the public restroom and poking his arm with another shard of broken glass. But he doesn't. He deprives himself of such luxury. He knows how he needs to sort this matter out before he does anything else; before he allows himself to truly and fully unwind.

His attention suddenly snaps to the sounds of two gentlemen shouting at one another further down the pathway. He spots a young, broad-shouldered man dressed in baggy, tattered clothing shouting at a middle-aged businessman wearing an expensive-looking suit. Although Enoch can barely make out the words of their shouting match because of the nearby traffic, he notices the young man pointing repeatedly at a lighter the businessman continues to flick open. He watches as the young man shrinks away whenever the older gentleman teases him with the lighter, brandishing the small flame in front of him. Finally, after what feels like hours, the young man skirts away from the businessman and begins to make his way up the path toward where Enoch is sitting.

For some reason, Enoch finds himself drawn to the young man. There's something so decidedly curious about him. He can't explain it, but he knows immediately that he must speak to the young man before he leaves.

The young man's pace slows to a crawl and eventually he arrives in Enoch's vicinity. Enoch straightens in his seat, preparing to speak. But he doesn't quite know what to say at first. The young man seems flustered, pacing back and forth in front of Enoch like a caged beast. Enoch's eyes beg the young man to look at him, but the young man doesn't seem to notice.

"Is everything okay?" Enoch finally asks.

The young man recoils, a little surprised. Whether he's astonished by Enoch's mere presence or that Enoch would care enough to ask, Enoch cannot be totally certain.

"Everything's fine, I suppose," the young man says, shrugging and looking away as if to make certain the businessman isn't still following him.

"Was that gentleman harassing you?" Enoch asks.

"If you could even call him a gentleman," the young man says, sneering. "I told him to not light his cigarette in front of me. I told him how I didn't care for the smoke. Or the way he used his lighter."

Enoch leans forward. "How did he use it—?"

"He flipped it open so carelessly," the young man says. "I thought the flame might—leap out and onto me."

The young man laughs, visibly uncomfortable.

"I know that's probably not likely," he says. "But once I got the idea in my head, I couldn't get it out. Ideas are tricky like that. If the mind is like a glue trap, then a bad idea is like a rat that gets caught there. For me at least, anyway."

Enoch nods, pretending to completely understand. "You don't care for smokers?"

"I don't care for the things that light them," the young man says, wincing so dramatically that Enoch wonders whether he's having a seizure. "I don't like fire. Anything that burns. It frightens me."

"You're scared of fire?" Enoch repeats.

"I know it sounds silly," the young man says, shrugging. "I've been afraid of it since I was a kid."

Enoch squints at the young man, realizing he's become a little too curious. "Did something happen to you when you were—?"

"Nothing happened," the young man shouts at him.

Enoch recoils, surprised by the young man's brashness. He collects himself and lets a comfortable silence settle between the two of them for a few moments.

"When you die, are you going to be cremated?" the young man asks him.

Enoch simpers, doing his best to contain his amusement at such an uncomfortable and morbid question.

"I don't think I've given it much thought," Enoch says. "Perhaps I should."

"I've made it very clear that I don't want to be cremated," the young man tells him. "I don't want to burn up. What if I'm cremated while still alive—?"

Enoch shrugs. "Of course, there's always the risk you could be buried alive."

"But I'm sure it doesn't compare to the agony of being burned alive," the young man says, shaking his head. "I'd never let them cremate me."

Just then, an idea arrives at the doorstep of Enoch's mind. *It's almost too easy*, he thinks to himself.

"You know, I suffer from the same apprehension," Enoch says to the young man.

His attention immediately snaps to Enoch, throwing him a distrustful glare.

Enoch gestures for him to sit. "Please."

The young man, a little tentative, drifts over to the bench and sits beside Enoch.

"I'm Enoch Leadbetter," Enoch says, offering his hand.

The young man accepts, shaking it. "Neville Breyman."

"Very pleased to meet you."

Neville forces an awkward smile. "You suffer from the same fear—?"

"All my life," Enoch explains. "Ever since I was a child. I used to go around the house and throw out all my mother's candles. She used to get so mad."

"It's the only sensible thing to do," Neville says, laughing and letting his guard down a little.

"I tried everything to overcome my fear," Enoch says. "I even tried hypnotherapy."

"Nothing worked—?"

Enoch grins sharply. "Something eventually did. Something I hadn't expected."

"What is it?" Neville asks, sliding further across the bench until his leg is pressed against Enoch's.

Enoch glances around, as if to make certain they're not being watched.

"If I show you, you must promise me you won't say anything," Enoch says to Neville.

"You're sure it works?" Neville asks him.

Enoch exhales an imitation of a sigh of relief. "It's offered my life back to me."

Neville thinks for a moment. Finally, he nods in agreement. "I won't say anything."

Without hesitation, Enoch reaches into the black bag between his feet and pulls out the large knife with the gilded handle. Neville instantly shrinks away at the sight of the weapon.

"Wait," he says. "What are you doing—?"

"You promised me," Enoch says.

Neville seems to realize Enoch is right because he immediately stifles himself, tightening his lips together as he watches Enoch without further comment.

Enoch rolls up his sleeve, exposing the small wound there. Neville's eyes are drawn to the tiny opening; however, he remains quiet. When he's satisfied with Neville's compliance, Enoch takes the knife and glides the edge of the blade along his forearm just below the other wound. A dark line of blood creeps there as the new wound yawns open like a budding plant. Enoch glances at Neville to make certain he's still watching. He smiles, noticing how Neville's attention is glued to the fresh wound.

"Now for my saving grace," Enoch tells him.

Enoch swipes the small purse from the bag, unravels the drawstring, and pulls out a small shard of glass. He pinches it between his thumb and index finger, wielding the glass in front of Neville as if it were a consecrated relic that Christ himself had once touched. Neville merely watches, wide-eyed in amazement.

Enoch then pushes the broken bit of glass inside the fresh wound until the tip completely vanishes, the sleeve of puckered tissue squelching as the glass stirs inside him. It's then that Enoch realizes how Neville continues to stare at him with his mouth open, clearly trying to comprehend the obscenity he just witnessed.

"Why would you do something like that?" Neville asks him.

"You don't approve?" Enoch asks.

"You told me it helped your fear," Neville says, his whole face souring. "It's—disgusting."

"Does glass burn?" Enoch asks Neville. "Tell me. Does it burn?"

Neville thinks for a moment. "I don't suppose it does."

"It's—what keeps me together, when I think of myself coming apart in the inferno," Enoch tells him. "I keep filling myself with broken bits of glass the same way a farmer might stuff a scarecrow. I think of all the parts of me that won't easily burn."

Neville bites his lower lip, clearly thinking. "And it works—?"

"I already told you," Enoch says.

Neville is quiet once more. He glances away from Enoch, his attention drifting to the noise of children playing in the grove of nearby trees with their parents. He gazes off, seemingly distant and dreaming for a few moments. Finally, his attention returns to Enoch.

"Will you let me try it—?" Neville asks.

Enoch responds by wiping his blood from the knife with a white cloth from his pocket. He motions for Neville to lift his sleeve. Neville obeys, exposing his arm and holding it out for Enoch to see properly.

"Now, this might hurt a little," Enoch warns him. "I promise to be gentle."

Before Neville can reply, Enoch slides the edge of the blade across his arm and blood wells up in the knife's path. Neville winces, squeezing his arm while he bleeds. Enoch snatches a new sliver of glass from the drawstring purse and flourishes it in front of Neville, secretly delighting in his torture. Finally, when Neville appears not to be able to bear it any longer, Enoch slides the broken bit of glass inside the wound he's opened in the young man's arm. Neville winces at the pain and then softens a little, as if surprised by the alarming pleasantness of the sensation. Enoch watches him for a moment, taking in the sight as Neville stirs in his seat and shifts like a spirited child.

"How does it feel?" Enoch asks.

Neville can scarcely bring himself to answer at first. Enoch notices how the young man's legs have tightened together, squeezing.

"It feels… I didn't think it was going to feel this way," Neville tells him.

"Are you thinking about fire?" Enoch asks.

A smile thaws across Neville's face as he comes to realize the truth. "No. Not until you just said the word. It's a… *beautiful* distraction."

"I told you," Enoch says, secretly delighting in being proven correct.

He can hardly believe it.

It worked, he thinks to himself. *I found the one.*

Before Neville drifts too far away into the ether of invisible ecstasy pluming all around him, Enoch takes hold of the young man's hand and squeezes tight. Severed from his trance, Neville's attention returns to Enoch as they sit together.

"There are some people I'd like you to meet," Enoch tells him.

FIVE

Enoch and Neville hardly speak to each other—let alone look at one other—as they make their way toward the small shop situated near the waterfront. Although Enoch entertains the prospect of initiating some semblance of polite conversation, everything he thinks of sounds entirely insipid or dull. Of course, he's curious about Neville—the young man in baggy clothing who seemed all too eager, a little too delighted to indulge in such an unusual and decidedly obscene fetish— but he still feels somewhat awkward in his presence despite the bond they had developed.

Finally, they arrive at the shop's entrance. Neville peers through one of the grime-covered windows, gazing inside the dimly lit store.

"A shop for cutlery?" he asks him.

Enoch doesn't answer. Instead, he pulls on the door handle and whisks the young man inside the store. The bell attached to the door chirps as they arrive, as if it were a tiny trumpet heralding their entrance. Enoch glances around the empty shop and surveys the rows of glass cases stretching to the rear of the store. A deafening silence lingers over the space and Enoch notices how Neville seems to shrink—as if feeling inadequate, as if decidedly feeling as though he did not belong there.

"Shall I ring the bell again—?" Neville asks, looking to Enoch for some sense of guidance.

"Wait," Enoch tells him, inching further and further into the shop.

Just then, the shopkeeper appears in the doorway at the end of the room. Neville shudders, a little startled at the sight.

"Mr. Leadbetter," the shopkeeper says warmly. "We thought you might not be joining us today. We started without you."

Enoch pushes Neville toward the shopkeeper. "I brought someone with me."

The shopkeeper eyes Neville up and down the way a snake might appraise its prey. "Certainly. I hope he brought his curiosity with him."

The shopkeeper motions for Enoch and Neville to follow him. Enoch and Neville obey, trailing after the shopkeeper until they arrive in the small room already filled with various well-dressed and immaculately manicured gentlemen and ladies. Enoch notices how Neville seems to whiten. Whether the poor thing feels underdressed because of his ragged clothing or whether he feels out of place because most of the guests are decidedly older than him, Enoch cannot be entirely certain.

The shopkeeper gestures for the both of them to sit and

they do, Neville's eyes avoiding the other group members.

Enoch observes as the shopkeeper takes to the center of the circle, addressing his guests with a warm welcome as he had yesterday. When it comes time for the group members to begin to undress, Neville looks at Enoch for an explanation. Enoch merely assures him with a benign look while rolling up one of his sleeves. Eventually, the shopkeeper arrives in front of Enoch with a small bit of broken glass in his open palm. Enoch accepts the offering with compassion and grace, his whole body tensing and threatening to explode when the shopkeeper slides the sliver of glass inside one of his open wounds.

Just as Enoch was neglected yesterday, the shopkeeper passes by Neville and doesn't offer a bit of glass to him. Neville, frowning, leans over to Enoch.

"I'm not allowed to join?" he asks him.

"You're not a member yet," Enoch whispers. "You're only able to receive the offering once you bring someone to recruit. Just like I did with you."

Enoch can't tell if Neville understands or if the poor young man feels a bit used and betrayed. Enoch reasons that Neville most likely feels a little bit of both.

After each guest has received their daily offering of glass, they begin to dress once more and file out of the room and head for the exit.

"Wait with me here," Enoch says to Neville, eyeing the shopkeeper from across the room.

The shopkeeper seems to notice Enoch's staring and makes his way over to him. Neville shrinks away as the shopkeeper approaches.

"Well done, Mr. Leadbetter," the shopkeeper says. "I was doubtful you'd arrange a recruit in such a short amount of time."

"Goes to show you that anything's possible," Enoch says, chuckling.

The shopkeeper's eyes narrow at Neville. "Mr. Leadbetter's explained the qualifications for joining our little community, young man?"

Neville swallows nervously. "Yes. He told me. I'm to bring someone new?"

"Someone who will appreciate our group," the shopkeeper says.

"Someone who knows pain, I take it," Neville says.

Enoch senses himself pale, a little surprised by Neville's morbid revelation.

"I guess you could say that," the shopkeeper says. "Are you up for the task?"

Neville thinks for a moment. Then he nods.

"You're in capable hands with Mr. Leadbetter as your guide," the shopkeeper says to the young man, patting him on the shoulder.

Before Neville or Enoch can utter another word, they find themselves being spirited toward the exit by the shopkeeper. He's waving at them, closing the door in their faces when they realize they've been delivered to the bustling street outside.

Enoch pulls his coat collar a little tighter around his neck. He looks overhead and notices how dark clouds have begun to drift toward them.

"Looks like it might rain again," Enoch says. "I suppose I

should catch a cab home."

Glancing at Neville out of the corner of his eye, he recognizes how the young man seems to stand without movement, as if he has been frozen there. His eyes avoid Enoch at all costs, his lips moving with muted words.

"Something wrong?" Enoch asks him, leaning closer and testing Neville's comfort.

"I—don't want to be alone right now," the young man says. "I don't want to go back to an empty room."

Surely, Enoch could understand. After all, he had spent enough time in empty rooms to know full well how devastatingly lonely they can be for a fragile soul. Enoch could tell, without a shadow of a doubt, that Neville was fragile. The poor young thing looks malnourished even, the vague outline of his rakishly thin frame hardly visible beneath his oversized clothing.

"My husband is hosting a dinner party tonight," Enoch tells him. "I'm afraid I don't have much time to spare."

"Just come back and have a drink, won't you?" Neville asks him. "Something to settle my nerves before I work up the courage to go out and find someone to recruit."

Enoch searches his mind for an excuse. When he realizes he has none to spare, he glares at Neville and nods in approval.

"A quick drink won't do much harm," Enoch says to him. "I can join you for a bit."

Neville's face softens, creasing with a polite smile.

"This way," he says, turning slightly and leading Enoch further up the street.

Enoch follows until something suddenly pains him—his arm. He senses the shard of glass stirring inside his open wound. Only this time, the agony isn't as exquisite as before. It's a dull, relentless ache that seems to tell him all at once that more suffering is on the way.

SIX

When Enoch arrives at Neville's cramped apartment, he searches his mind for pleasantries to share—polite conversation to make while Neville hastens to the kitchenette and begins to prepare the drinks. Enoch feels immediately unsettled, surveying the small living space and how the floor is littered with various cardboard boxes and half-empty takeout containers. He notices how some of the lamps in the room are outfitted with brightly colored Chinese paper lanterns and he simpers a little, amused at the absurd thought of Neville attempting to make the squalid little room look moderately presentable to guests. Enoch figures Neville doesn't entertain friends very often, especially given how unsafe the neighborhood seemed as they walked through it.

Neville encourages Enoch to take a seat on the couch and says he'll bring him a drink as soon as he opens the bottle of whiskey, but Enoch finds himself struggling to locate an area to sit that hasn't already been piled with unwashed clothing. Finally, Enoch uncovers a place to sit and does so. He tightens his grip about the black bag with the knife inside. He glances inside the bag and notices the drawstring purse filled with shards of glass that the shopkeeper had given him.

"Perhaps we should add another bit of glass today—?" Enoch asks Neville, swiping the drawstring purse and pulling it open. "It calms me down."

Neville approaches Enoch with a small glass filled with whiskey.

"Let's wait first," the young man says to him. "I'm— feeling a bit out of place right now."

Enoch finds it unusual that Neville might confess to something so bizarre. After all, it's his apartment. Why should he feel so out of place in his own home?

"A sliver of broken glass might help," Enoch says, teasing him with the small purse of broken bits. "I think it would make you feel better."

For a moment, Neville gazes at Enoch. Enoch winces, a little unsettled by Neville's scrupulous glare.

"You know, I'm glad I met you," Neville says to him. "I've always had a difficult time meeting others, connecting with people. You know—?"

Of course, Enoch could understand. He stirs quietly in his seat, fully prepared to allow Neville to speak as much as he'd like.

"People tend not to want to linger around me unless I make them," Neville explains. "I don't know how to make anyone care for me the same way I care for them."

Enoch tenses, a little worried by Neville's confession. After all, why is he sharing something so decidedly personal? It's not that Enoch isn't opposed to Neville becoming so vulnerable; however, it seems so improper given how recently they've connected.

Perhaps this is why you can't make anyone stay in your company, Enoch thinks to himself. *Too eager to share things— things that don't need to be divulged.*

"You probably think I'm silly for confessing something so… ridiculous," Neville says, his tone firming a little.

Enoch tries to force a laugh but can't for some reason. He tries to shift one of his fingers on his right hand and finds every possibility of movement completely deadened. The whole room begins to blur, and Enoch lets the glass of whiskey slip from his grasp, shattering against the floor. Neville merely stares at Enoch, observing him with a vacant look—an inevitable, almost hate-filled look. Enoch urges his body to lift from the couch, but movement is now impossible. All he can do is sink further back into the couch until he's totally immobile—his limbs completely paralyzed.

He regards Neville with a questioning look, begging him to explain what's happening to him. Enoch flexes his lips, struggling to speak. All he can utter are grunts and groans, involuntary noises like when an infant babbles.

"I'd like to show you something," Neville says to Enoch, straightening from his seat and moving across the room toward what appears to be the door to a broom closet. "I've been thinking about who I could recruit. I've thought about who might find themselves enraptured with the community you've found for me."

Enoch's jaw slackens, his mouth hanging open as drool begins to ooze from between his lips. He tries to say something again, but all he can muster is an impassioned grunt. Neville seems to laugh at his anguish, delighting in his visible discomfort.

"I've been eager to introduce you to my companion since we first met," Neville explains, twisting the handle and pulling the closet door open.

Peering inside the dimly lit space, he motions to something—someone—stirring in the dark corner where the two walls meet.

"Come out, my beloved," Neville whispers. "We're waiting for you."

Enoch's eyes widen in disbelief as a dark shape wrenches itself from inside the closet and out into the light. It crawls on all fours the way an animal would, its head lowered as if out of respect for its superiors. It isn't long before Enoch makes the horrible realization that the dark shape—the pathetic creature slinking on all fours—is a middle-aged naked man with a shaved head. Enoch nearly retches when the poor man's miserable face comes into full view. The man's eyes—sunken craters of blistered tissue, half-melted as if someone had held a blowtorch there. His nose—a gaping wound, the edges of the opening scabbed dark red as if it had been cauterized. Finally, and perhaps most obscene of all: the poor thing's skin—speckled all over with oozing black welts, as though someone had held a lighter against his bare flesh time and time again.

The man on all fours cowers a little when Neville draws near, the same way a dog that's been trained to be fearful of its owner might. Enoch watches in silence as Neville pats the man's head like a hunter rewarding a bloodhound for discovering fresh prey.

"I think the group will welcome him with open arms, don't you?" Neville asks Enoch, chuckling a little as if knowing full well that Enoch could never answer. "Of course, I'll have to give him a bath before we attend the meeting tomorrow."

Enoch watches in horror as the man crawling on all fours brushes his head against Neville's knee, as if demanding to be petted again. Neville complies, scratching the man beneath his bearded chin.

Then Neville approaches Enoch and drags him from the chair until he's spread out on the floor like slaughtered offal. Enoch tries to resist, but there's nothing that can be done. He merely flops there like a rag doll as he lands on the ground, Neville beginning to undress him. Peeling his shirt from him, Neville exposes Enoch's arm with the identical fresh wounds. The man on all fours draws near, sniffing Enoch's head, but Neville swats him away.

Enoch is surprised when Neville pulls out a lighter from his pocket. Neville flips the lighter open, a small flame flickering to life.

"It usually takes my mind off it when I burn other things," Neville explains to Enoch. "But I've found that things—people—waste away after a while. Fire devours everything."

Enoch senses tears webbing in the corners of his eyes as

he blinks, understanding the untold agonies that Neville has in store for him.

"But not you," Neville says. "You're already filled with bits of glass that won't burn. I'll be able to keep you around for a while."

Smiling from ear to ear, Neville grabs hold of Enoch's paralyzed arm and begins to bring the flame down against the small wound filled with broken bits of glass. He holds it there for a moment until Enoch's skin begins to sizzle and crisp black like a tube of overcooked sausage. Enoch feels every horrible sensation, his mouth remaining open in a God-awful, silent scream.

When Neville is satisfied with the work he's done on Enoch's first wound, he moves to the other. As Neville holds the flame there, pushing it further and further against Enoch's blistering wound, Enoch begins to sense his toes curling. He's surprised when he realizes he can command them to move on their own. Like a tide leaching throughout his body, the possibility of movement slowly returns to him bit by bit. His arms and legs still feel heavy, as if they were pinned beneath concrete weights; however, he suddenly senses how his jaw can move more freely, his lips flexing with newfound liberty.

Neville seems to recognize Enoch's bewilderment and draws closer to him. Enoch strains to say something to him, but he still can't utter the words.

"What's that, my pet—?" Neville asks, leaning a little closer.

Just as Neville pushes his head against Enoch's face,

Enoch lurches up and clamps his teeth down on Neville's ear. Neville screams, surprised, as Enoch bites down and rips off his ear. Blood hosing the both of them in a dark tide, Neville clutches the side of his head and scrambles to his feet. As Neville pulls himself away, shouting in distress, Enoch slowly pulls himself off the ground and gathers himself. He watches as the man crawling on all fours begins to pace the room like a stressed animal. Then he notices how Neville has already limped into the kitchenette, swiping a dishrag from the counter, and pressing it against his bleeding head. Without hesitation, Enoch roots in the black bag and pulls out the large knife with the gilded handle. Taking it from the bag, he staggers after Neville and raises the knife high.

Neville cowers, holding his arms up as if they were his only defense, when Enoch brings the knife down hard and slashes through the young man's pathetic protection. Slicing Neville's hand open until the fingers disconnect and snap like rubber bands, Enoch then drives the knife into Neville's face again and again, until the crimson wellspring buried between Neville's eyes finally explodes and fountains Enoch with a blood-red hailstorm that breaks against him like a crashing wave. Enoch watches in silence as Neville collapses to the ground—his hands sliced to confetti and his face now nothing more than a gaping crater pumping out a steady stream of dark crimson.

Enoch admires his handiwork for a moment—surprised at himself, surprised he could do something so awful, so grotesque.

Finally peeling himself away from the mess he's made of Neville in the kitchenette, Enoch staggers into the living room, where he finds the man kneeling near the front door, as if waiting for Enoch the way a dog waits for its owner to let him outside.

Enoch twists the door handle and pushes it open, the naked man crawling out on all fours and onto the empty street. Enoch wonders if the man will scamper off the way all freed animals seem to. But he's surprised when the pathetic creature waits for him there, whimpering a little as if begging Enoch to join him.

Clutching the knife in his hand, Enoch limps out of the small apartment and makes his way into the street. He admits to himself how he might be quite a sight—his face nothing more than a mask of gore, his gaping wounds, his weak limp. And then, of course, there's the man crawling beside him every step of the way back home—his small, naked form pockmarked with various cuts, his skin coated with dirt and grime, his face as awful as the headliner of a sideshow attraction.

Together, they meander along the city streets, people stepping aside and studying them in total horror as they approach and then drift further away. Enoch doesn't seem to hear the shouts from others as they pass. He doesn't pay attention to the commotion that seems to boom whenever both he and his new friend are in the vicinity of people who don't understand the agony they've endured.

Finally, after an hour or so, Enoch and the man crawling on all fours arrive at Enoch's apartment building. It's late in the evening and Enoch fully expects his husband to be entertaining their guests.

He twists the key into the lock and forces the door open, slinking into the apartment, where he's immediately greeted with a room filled with dear friends. They all seem to pale, eyes widening in terror, as they observe Enoch shuffle out from the shadows and into the light with the naked man crawling beside him. Enoch searches the small crowd for a sign of his husband. Cedric finally comes into view, weaving between guests and beginning to approach Enoch with a cautiousness he's clearly never practiced before.

Enoch says nothing at first, his eyes donating a listless, vacant stare as he tightens his grip around the knife's handle.

"Darling?" Cedric says, gently approaching Enoch as he stands there framed in the open doorway.

The naked man curled at Enoch's side like a loving, obedient pet begins to growl at Cedric as he draws nearer. Cedric, paling, backs away.

"What happened?" Cedric asks his husband.

Enoch doesn't say anything at first. He answers, passing the blood-buttered knife into Cedric's hands. Cedric nearly retches at the sight, blood dripping from the edge of the blade.

Then Enoch laughs, as if on the verge of sobbing—as if the agony, the anguish could come spilling out from him in a horrific geyser at any moment.

The guests separate as Enoch weaves through the small crowd, making his way toward the dining room table littered with empty plates and glasses. He snatches a wine glass and, without warning, smashes it against the table until the broken bits skate across the floor toward Cedric's feet. Whispers filter throughout the small crowd of friends, clearly bewildered and unsure what to do. Enoch kneels, plucking one of the bits of glass from the ground and admiring it for a moment.

"And to think," Enoch says, sliding the sliver of broken glass inside his wound and tensing for a moment until he finally softens. "All this for a knife."

PRICKLE

"Big deal. Death always went with the territory. I'll see you in Disneyland."

Richard Ramirez (US serial killer on being sentenced to death)

It had been nearly ten years since Mr. Arthur Spirro had laid eyes on Mr. Emmett Chessler, their interactions limited to greeting cards during the holiday season and the occasional telephone call when it was permitted.

Mr. Spirro found himself out of sorts as he idled there in the sunny June weather, wondering if age had robbed his dear friend of all his wit, charm, and perspicacity. Of course, Mr. Chessler had always been sharp and impeccable when it came to social graces; however, Mr. Spirro reasoned that ten years was a considerable amount of time and provided ample opportunity to bleach away the fine character of a man he had always held in such high esteem.

To say that Mr. Spirro idolized Mr. Chessler would be incorrect and especially unfitting seeing as the two had spent nearly every Saturday together in Mayweather Park, before Mr. Chessler's family had sent him abroad to convalesce due to a medical concern—a minor palpitation of the heart that caused the poor man to twitch involuntarily. Mr. Chessler had told Mr. Spirro of his embarrassment and how he loathed the involuntary spasms he endured day in and day out. Of course, Mr. Spirro had told his friend not to worry and that his family were well within the realm of appropriateness to show concern for a man in his sixties.

However, now that ten years had passed since Mr. Chessler's tremors first occurred, both Mr. Spirro and Mr. Chessler were much older and were now gentlemen in their seventies. Mr. Spirro figured he had kept himself in adequate shape. Naturally, his gut had remained an issue seeing as he indulged in elaborate cuisine on more than one occasion each week. However, for the most part, Mr. Spirro conceded he was a picture of health. He hoped and prayed Mr. Chessler had maintained the same level of inflexibility with regard to his well-being. After all, now that Mr. Chessler had returned to the sanctity of his family's home in Portsmouth, New Hampshire, Mr. Spirro hoped that the two of them could resume their weekly afternoon meetings in Mayweather Park.

While Mr. Spirro lazed on the park bench, the hot summer sun beating down on him, he thought of the last time he and Mr. Chessler had met before his friend was sent abroad to recuperate.

"The Spanish sun will put some color in your cheeks," Mr. Spirro had told him, noticing the poor man's resentment at the fact he had to be sent away like some irritable schoolboy. "Barcelona is charming this time of year. You'll eat the finest foods. Drink the finest wines. I can't pretend I'm not envious. You must write to me."

But Mr. Chessler hadn't appeared persuaded. Instead, he had faltered for a moment, his lips parting as if daring to say something that begged for eons to be finally uttered.

It was then that Mr. Chessler had done something that surprised Mr. Spirro terribly and had caused him to pull away in shock. Mr. Chessler had pushed his hand against Mr. Spirro's and squeezed tight the way young lovers do.

"I wish you could join," Mr. Chessler had told him, regarding his friend with such longing, such indescribable aching. "I'd give anything to take you with me."

Of course, it wasn't long before Mr. Chessler had pulled away and rested his hands in his lap, that ravenous look of yearning slowly dissolving from his eyes.

Mr. Spirro often thought of that moment and wondered what it had truly meant. Naturally, he and Mr. Chessler had grown very close—somewhat attached—in the years leading up to Mr. Chessler's departure. However, it had been the very first time Mr. Chessler had displayed a semblance of vulnerability. Moreover, it was the first time Mr. Chessler had strained to touch Mr. Spirro. The heat of Mr. Chessler's skin felt unusual and yet somehow sublime to Mr. Spirro. He conceded that it was a charming moment. Of course, Mr. Chessler could have been somewhat maudlin about his inevitable departure; however, something deep inside Mr. Spirro whispered to him that there was another reason for the man's look of craving—a reason that perhaps was the motivation for his family to send him away. Mr. Spirro wondered if Mr. Chessler harbored feelings for him. Perhaps not the same lascivious feelings as between two sexual partners; however, the same sentiment lingered in the air. After all, Mr. Spirro could scarcely forget that look of desire in Mr. Chessler's eyes right before he left—that intense look of unrequited passion that flickered in the poor man's eyes like brightly burning streetlamps.

What could he have meant? Mr. Spirro wondered to himself, his attention occasionally drifting to the group of families milling about the nearby gated park entrance. *Did he mean that he wished he could up and run away with me? Surely, his family would disapprove.*

It was then that Mr. Spirro was reminded of Mr. Chessler's overbearing and equally overassertive daughter, Rebecca. He recalled how Mr. Chessler once confided in him how Rebecca had detested his weekly meetings with Mr. Spirro, how she berated him and begged him to stay home. There was a part of Mr. Spirro that wondered if Rebecca somehow suspected her father of his seemingly unnatural feelings. Of course, it wasn't completely out of the question for Mr. Chessler to harbor feelings for someone. After all, his wife, Bethany, had been dead for five years when he and Mr. Spirro first met at a reception at the local art museum.

Still, Mr. Chessler's daughter was entirely dismissive of her father's yearning to visit the park each Saturday to meet with Mr. Spirro. Mr. Chessler had told Mr. Spirro how Rebecca had made little efforts to impede his visits. Despite her regular interference, Mr. Chessler had shown up at two o'clock each Saturday afternoon with the adeptness of a German train schedule—always and forever devoted to his friend: Mr. Spirro.

But today was different. Of course, Mr. Spirro expected Mr. Chessler's return to be somewhat dissimilar to their previous rendezvous, especially given the poor man's health; however, Mr. Spirro began to grow worried as time passed and Mr. Chessler was nowhere to be found.

The dear man certainly couldn't have forgotten, Mr. Spirro thought to himself. *We agreed on the phone to meet at our usual spot at our usual time.*

Mr. Spirro wondered if perhaps Rebecca had made an effort to prevent Mr. Chessler from arriving. After all, what was Mr. Chessler to do with regard to his daughter? Mr. Spirro had no children but figured that any parent would be devoted to the wishes of their offspring. Mr. Spirro decided he would wait another five minutes before departing.

Thankfully for Mr. Spirro, only three minutes passed before he noticed a small elderly man weaving along the pathway that circled the lake across from where he was seated. Mr. Spirro had wondered to himself if he would recognize Mr. Chessler when he first arrived, and he was delighted to find that he immediately took notice of him and observed the red carnation decorating the old man's breast pocket. He was impressed with his own eyesight, considering the fact that Mr. Chessler was a few hundred yards away when Mr. Spirro first caught a glimpse of him.

Mr. Chessler was smaller than Mr. Spirro remembered. The poor thing meandered along with the impeccable cautiousness of a cleric, afraid to displease some kind of invisible superior that might immediately find fault with him.

As the old man drew closer, Mr. Spirro noticed how

more lines and wrinkles had gathered across Mr. Chessler's visible skin. He noticed how Mr. Chessler's mouth seemed to permanently pull downward, as if prepared to divulge bad news at any given moment. Perhaps the most curious addition to Mr. Chessler's appearance was a dark scar that ran from his left eyebrow to below his cheek and near his lips—the thin ribbon of skin rusted brown like an unraveled thread. Mr. Spirro recoiled slightly at the sight, immediately taken aback by the wound Mr. Chessler seemed to display so proudly. Even more unusual, the scar looked somewhat recent and appeared as if it hadn't been cleaned or dressed properly.

As Mr. Spirro collected himself, Mr. Chessler approached and was eventually within a few feet.

"Arthur—?" the old man asked, adjusting his eyewear, and leaning his glasses to the tip of his nose.

Mr. Spirro forced a smile and shot up from the bench. "Emmett, dear friend."

He offered his hand, and they shook. Mr. Spirro hesitated slightly, noticing how frail and delicate Mr. Chessler had become. The old man's hand felt rubbery and elastic.

Mr. Spirro patted Mr. Chessler on both shoulders. "You look well."

Of course, it was a lie. But Mr. Spirro hoped he sounded convincing.

"Time abroad has done you wonders," Mr. Spirro told him. "I'll have to schedule my holiday in Barcelona next year. I'll bet you had a marvelous time."

Mr. Chessler smirked a little, as if not wanting to say one thing or the other.

"It's good to be home," he said. "I've missed this place."

"It's missed you, dear friend," Mr. Spirro told him. "Here. Sit and join me. Like old times."

Mr. Spirro motioned for Mr. Chessler to sit beside him on the bench. Mr. Chessler accepted politely, sitting near Mr. Spirro but not as close as they once did. Mr. Spirro wondered if Mr. Chessler's positioning on the bench was deliberate or if it was something he did somewhat absentmindedly. Regardless, it didn't matter now that Mr. Chessler was finally present. He was here and that was all that mattered.

There was an uncomfortable silence hanging over them almost instantly. Mr. Spirro swallowed nervously, wondering what to say. After all, what could be said after nearly ten years? There was so much to say and then again so little to be said. They might as well have been strangers meeting for the very first time.

"You'll have to tell me all about the exceptional Spanish cuisine you've been eating," Mr. Spirro said, always more than eager to discuss food. "Even though I'm sure my skin will turn green with envy the moment I hear you describe some of the wines you must have sampled."

Mr. Chessler adjusted his collar slightly, his throat flexing. "The doctors usually discouraged me from drinking any wine, I'm afraid. You might be surprised to know that I've been living like some sort of Cistercian monk for the past several years."

"I know all about doctor's orders," Mr. Spirro said. "Better to be safe than sorry."

Once again, an uncomfortable silence lingered over the

two of them. Mr. Spirro tried to think of things to say, but everything seemed so artificial, so stupidly calculated that he knew for certain Mr. Chessler would see right through his pretense. More than anything, he wanted his friend to feel comfortable. It couldn't have been easy, after all— living all those years in a strange, foreign country because family members had sent him away like a problem to be fixed by doctors. Of course, it was entirely possible that Mr. Chessler was healthier for it now; however, Mr. Spirro wasn't completely convinced yet.

"How's your daughter Rebecca?" he asked Mr. Chessler.

The old man shrugged a little with the disinterest of a sullen teenager. "She's fine, I suppose. Hovers too much. She always did that. You know."

"Yes," Mr. Spirro said. "You told me how she always… *worried* about you."

Mr. Chessler's eyes pulled downward with a look of resentment. "Still does, I'm afraid."

"You look well enough," Mr. Spirro said. "Surely, some of her concern must be… misdirected."

It was then that Mr. Spirro glanced down and noticed how the skin around Mr. Chessler's fingernails was raw, blistered, and red—as if he had been relentlessly biting and picking at them.

"She and her husband want to send me back," Mr. Chessler confessed. "Not to Barcelona, however. They've been in touch with a doctor in Norway. They're trying to convince me to go. But who knows for how long?"

Mr. Spirro, of course, had expected this. He wondered

if Mr. Chessler desperately needed the medical care. After all, in the few moments they had been together, he noticed how Mr. Chessler's right eye involuntarily twitched. He had also noticed how his hands seemed to tremor slightly as well. Perhaps this was for the best.

"I suppose if they think it will do you good to go," Mr. Spirro said. "How could you argue with that?"

Mr. Chessler seemed to notice how Mr. Spirro was staring at his blistered fingernails and immediately tucked them beneath his armpits so they were out of sight.

"I can't begin to tell you how much I loathe living abroad," Mr. Chessler told him. "It's nearly unbearable."

Mr. Spirro softened a little, hoping his calmness would ease his friend. "I'm sure it takes some getting used to. But if it's for the best—"

"I know what's for the best," Mr. Chessler told him, cutting him off.

Mr. Spirro regarded him with a wordless question, uncertain if he wanted to actually know the answer.

"I'd give anything to bring you with me," the old man said. "To know that you were there. That you'd look after me. You'd take care of me."

Mr. Spirro hesitated. He could hardly believe Mr. Chessler was revealing himself once more to him. Everything Mr. Spirro had suspected was true—Mr. Chessler was deeply in love with him. He knew it. He saw it in the way Mr. Chessler regarded him with such envy and longing. He heard it in the way his voice seemed to lilt slightly whenever the old man was in his presence. Of course, Mr. Spirro was flattered. However, there was something wrong—he felt no similar feelings for Mr. Chessler. Even if he was of a similar persuasion, Mr. Spirro knew in his heart that the two of them were never to belong together. They were friends and nothing more. How could Mr. Chessler make every effort to dismantle the dear friendship they had come to build over the years?

"Arthur, there's something I need to tell you," Mr. Chessler said, leaning uncomfortably close to Mr. Spirro.

Mr. Spirro, of course, knew exactly what Mr. Chessler was about to say. He had dreaded this moment many times before; however, he could hardly believe it was happening. He knew he had to think of something that would divert Mr. Chessler for the entirety of their visit together. Then, once they had departed, he could resign himself to the fact that Mr. Chessler did care for him in such a way and he could think of a plan to make it known to his friend that his longing was appreciated and yet totally inappropriate.

Finally, something came to him.

"Emmett, do you recall that game we used to play with one another?" Mr. Spirro asked, straightening in his seat. "It was one of our favorite things to do whenever we met…"

Mr. Chessler looked bewildered at first. Perhaps he was a little upset that Mr. Spirro had changed the subject so rapidly; however, he didn't seem upset enough to continue what he was saying. He seemed to give in to Mr. Spirro's whim at the drop of a hat.

"Yes," Mr. Chessler said. "I remember the game quite well. One of our more… *macabre* inventions."

"What did we call it?" Mr. Spirro asked him, pretending

to momentarily forget. "We had a name for it, didn't we?"

Mr. Chessler thought for a moment, visibly searching his mind for the answer. Finally, it came to him.

"*Prickle*," he said, his lips threatening to curl with a smile.

"Good memory," Mr. Spirro said. "Better than mine, that's for certain. Do you remember why we called it *Prickle*?"

"From the definition of the word," Mr. Chessler told him. "It's when you experience a tingling sensation. Like the hairs on the back of your neck standing up."

"You recall the rules?" Mr. Spirro asked.

Mr. Chessler laughed. "Surely, you can't expect me to remember *everything*."

"But you certainly recollect the purpose of the unusual exercise."

Mr. Chessler thought for a moment, as if selecting his words very carefully. "I suppose it was to inconvenience others."

Mr. Spirro nodded. "More to the point: to perform little cruelties on people we don't know and we'll never see ever again."

A smile leached across Mr. Chessler's face. He regarded Mr. Spirro with such unreserved curiosity.

"Was there a reason you brought that up?" he asked him.

Mr. Spirro shrugged slightly. "Perhaps we should play a round for old times' sake. Especially if you say you'll be leaving again soon."

Mr. Chessler's eyes lowered once more with a look of mournfulness. "I haven't played that wonderful game in years."

"Not since we saw each other last?" Mr. Spirro asked him.

But Mr. Spirro was surprised when Mr. Chessler shook his head slightly.

"No," the old man told him. "There was another time. When I was living abroad. I played it with a gentleman I had met at the opera. But I'm afraid things didn't go as planned."

Mr. Chessler's attention suddenly drifted far and away, as if his very soul had been sucked out of his body through the valve of his open mouth. He remained like this for several moments before eventually returning and throwing a glance at Mr. Spirro.

"Shall we play?" Mr. Spirro asked him.

Mr. Chessler glanced around him, studying each passerby—each unfamiliar face, each day to be ruined. "But who to begin with?"

It was then that Mr. Spirro took note of an elderly woman seated on a bench a few hundred yards away from where they were sitting. She was leaning forward in her chair and offering breadcrumbs to the small ducks that were floating near the water's edge. Occasionally, she'd wrench her attention from the wildlife and would nod in acknowledgment of the ladies and gentlemen passing by her.

Mr. Spirro nudged Mr. Chessler's shoulder and pointed to the old woman across the small causeway.

"A relatively simple target," Mr. Spirro told his friend. "After all, you've been out of practice for so long."

Mr. Chessler snorted and then composed himself. "What shall I do to her?"

Without hesitation, Mr. Spirro reached into his pocket

and pulled out a small kit with his initials embossed on the side. He flipped the case open and out popped a tray filled with all the necessary equipment for facial grooming and cuticle care. Mr. Chessler eyed him with wonder as Mr. Spirro plucked a small blackhead extractor from the kit and brandished it in front of him.

"I'm afraid I suffer from a most unfortunate affliction," Mr. Spirro told his friend. "Horrible blackheads. Not very becoming. Clustered especially on the tip of my nose. I use this to squeeze and pop them open. It's fitting: that's exactly what you're going to do to that dear woman—pop her open. But ever so gently."

Mr. Spirro noticed how Mr. Chessler's eyes widened at him.

"What do you want me to do?" Mr. Chessler asked him.

Mr. Spirro flipped the curve of the blackhead extractor over and revealed a needlepoint lancet on the other end of the instrument. The tip was dagger sharp and as thin as a sewing needle. In the right hands, it could obviously do a considerable amount of damage.

"See how sharp this is?" Mr. Spirro asked Mr. Chessler. "It's tiny but lethal, I assure you. I want you to take care while using it."

Mr. Spirro passed the needlepoint lancet into Mr. Chessler's hands. Mr. Chessler admired the small weapon for a moment and then brought his attention to Mr. Spirro once more.

"You want me to—?"

"Charm her," Mr. Spirro told him. "Charm her with the

same wit and sophistication that struck me those many years ago when I first met you. Then, once you've wormed your way into her trust, take the lancet and poke her arm."

Mr. Chessler shook his head. "What if she cries out?"

"She certainly might, dear friend," Mr. Spirro said. "Tell her it was a wasp. I'm sure you'll be able to convince her of anything if she's especially smitten with you."

Mr. Chessler regarded the instrument once more, his attention glued to the device and seemingly imagining each and every horrible scenario that could happen.

"I—don't know," he said. "It could be dangerous."

"My dear friend, that's the joy of *Prickle*," Mr. Spirro told him. "The thrill of being caught. The joy in ruining someone else's day. Don't you remember any of it?"

Mr. Chessler thought carefully.

"Yes. I suppose I do," he said, gripping the extractor a little tighter and with a little more confidence.

"Then go on," Mr. Spirro said. "Let's see if you can still charm snakes."

Mr. Spirro patted Mr. Chessler on the back so forcefully that it propelled the poor man forward. He staggered to his feet and composed himself, clearly worried that others were somehow observing him and marking his performance. Mr. Spirro watched as Mr. Chessler, with great hesitation, began to amble across the pathway toward the elderly woman sitting alone on the park bench beside the riverbank. Thankfully, the old woman was close enough that Mr. Spirro could overhear anything and intervene if things got out of hand.

Mr. Spirro watched as Mr. Chessler meandered toward her, skirting around the edge of the pathway, and observing her with such care and dedication. Mr. Chessler glanced back at Mr. Spirro, as if begging him for a look of assurance. But there was none to be had. Mr. Spirro merely sat there and watched without expression.

Finally, after several moments of dawdling, Mr. Chessler circled the bench and came into the old woman's peripheral vision at the river's edge where the small ducks were gathered.

"The water must be warm for them this time of year," Mr. Chessler said to her. "Must be like soaking in a nice, hot bath."

The old woman smiled, nodding. "Would you like to take some crumbs to feed them?"

Mr. Chessler hesitated slightly, glancing at Mr. Spirro and then back at the old woman. She brandished the bag in front of him as an offering. Mr. Chessler reached inside and pulled out several bits of bread. He thanked her for the small kindness and then drifted closer to the water's edge, flicking the breadcrumbs at the ducks as they continued to bob in the shallow water.

"I don't believe I've seen you here before," the old woman said to him.

Mr. Chessler turned. His eyes darted to Mr. Spirro and then back to the elderly woman staring at him.

"I used to come here quite frequently," he told her, shoving his hands into his pockets. "Every Saturday at two in the afternoon. Just like clockwork. But I've been away for a while. Living abroad. I thought it might be fun to return to the place where I was always the happiest."

"I'm happy here too," the old woman said. "I used to bring my daughter here when she was little to feed the ducks. But she finally moved away, and I don't see her much anymore."

Mr. Chessler glanced at the empty spot on the bench beside the old woman.

"May I?" he asked her.

"By all means," she said, swiping her leather handbag and setting it on the ground beside her feet. "I'm always so hopeful that someone will join me. But usually it's just families in the park on Saturday. They don't pay an old woman a second glance."

"I'm glad to hear you don't mind an old man joining you," Mr. Chessler said to her.

Mr. Spirro smiled as he watched the two of them from afar. Of course, Mr. Chessler was slightly out of practice, and Mr. Spirro assumed the old woman could tell that his dear friend was uneasy around her; however, it didn't matter now. The two of them were seated together and chatting amicably like old friends who had been parted for several years. In fact, their conversation seemed so natural that Mr. Chessler's nerves seemed to be dissipating by the second.

"I was surprised to find you sitting so close to the water here," Mr. Chessler told her.

The old woman regarded him queerly, eyes squinting at him. "I don't know what you mean."

"A lot of the children that play here leave their candy

wrappers near the water's edge. It attracts all sorts of bugs. But especially wasps in the summertime."

The old woman glanced around, clearly bewildered. "I haven't seen any wasps today. Hardly ever."

"Consider yourself fortunate," Mr. Chessler said to her, dipping his hand into the pocket where he had slid the needlepoint lancet.

"Oh, dear," he whispered, eyeing her suddenly with such uninhibited concern.

The old woman seemed to pale immediately, shrinking from him. "My God, what is it?"

"There's one floating right beside your shoulder," he said to her, eyes locked on the pretend insect. "Be very still. Close your eyes."

The old woman obeyed without comment.

Mr. Chessler drew closer and closer, pulling the lancet from his pocket and preparing it for the task at hand. When he was certain the time had finally come, he poked her arm with the lancet and immediately drew away, flicking the instrument into the nearby underbrush.

The old woman shrieked and all heads in the park swiveled in their direction.

Mr. Spirro straightened from his seat, preparing to intervene if necessary. Thankfully, Mr. Chessler had the prescience to avoid a scene and wave several onlookers away while he comforted the old woman.

"Did the damn thing sting you?" he asked her.

"Yes," she cried out, clutching her arm. "You were right. I never saw it."

"It was my fault," Mr. Chessler told her. "I swatted at it, and I must have upset it. Are you alright?"

The old woman's face soured as she continued to cradle her stung arm. "I suppose so."

"You aren't allergic, are you?" Mr. Chessler asked.

"No, I'll be fine," the old woman assured him, shaking her head. "I'm just so surprised. I never even saw the thing near me. Never even heard it."

"They're quick and they're temperamental, I'm afraid," Mr. Chessler said.

Then he glanced back at Mr. Spirro, who was already waving him to abandon the old woman and return to him.

Mr. Chessler cleared his throat. "You don't need medical attention or anything, do you?"

The old woman waved him away. "No. I think I'll be okay. It just hurt a little."

"I hope you'll excuse me," Mr. Chessler said. "I'm rather allergic and I'd like to avoid it, if possible."

"Yes, of course," the old woman told him, a little visibly surprised by his sudden mention of departure. "I understand."

"Perhaps I'll see you again here?" he asked her.

"Without the wasps, I hope," she said.

They laughed and then Mr. Chessler excused himself, meandering up the grassy knoll toward the bench where Mr. Spirro was seated like a deity presiding over all earthly mortals.

"Did you see it?" Mr. Chessler asked, throwing himself onto the bench beside his friend. "I doubted I would go through with it."

Mr. Spirro held out his hand. "Where's the extractor?"

Mr. Chessler eyed him with a look of regret.

"Well—?"

"I had to throw it away after I poked her," Mr. Chessler confessed. "I was afraid she'd see it."

"The damn thing was expensive," Mr. Spirro told him. "You threw it away?"

"How was I?" Mr. Chessler asked him. "I realize I'm out of practice, but I'd say it was fairly successful."

Swallowing some of his concern about his lost extractor, Mr. Spirro patted his friend on the shoulder. "It was— marvelous. I was very impressed. The perfect little cruelty. Without any of the consequences."

"I hope I didn't hurt her too much," Mr. Chessler said, biting his fingernails. "I was a little too zealous with the poke, I'm afraid. I think she might have bled some. Thankfully, she didn't seem to notice at the time."

"Perhaps she'll think twice before she sits on that bench again," Mr. Spirro told him.

Then Mr. Chessler's attention turned to Mr. Spirro.

"I guess that means it's finally your turn," he said, smiling a little too devotedly.

"I suppose that's true," Mr. Spirro told him. "What shall I do?"

Mr. Spirro watched as Mr. Chessler's attention drifted from passerby to passerby, assessing each possibility and welcoming the thought of bringing them such unreserved cruelty. It was then that Mr. Spirro noticed Mr. Chessler's attention fixed on a middle-aged gentleman ambling along further down the pathway. He was aided by a wooden cane with a silver handle. The man limped along, others weaving around him and eyeing him as if he were a nuisance. Finally, he located a nearby empty bench and sat.

Mr. Chessler pointed at the man with the cane and turned to Mr. Spirro.

"Snap his cane in half," he said to him.

Mr. Spirro hesitated for a moment. He wondered if Mr. Chessler was capable of ever truly crossing an invisible line of decency. Of course, the game was depraved and that was the intention of its existence, as a way for the two of them to pass the time in the park on Saturday afternoons. However, Mr. Spirro couldn't help but wonder if Mr. Chessler delighted in the torture, the humiliation of others. He wondered if Mr. Chessler secretly relished these cruelties and wished they could inflict more misery upon their unsuspecting victims.

"You want me to break that man's walking equipment?" Mr. Spirro asked him. Just to be certain. "What if he falls and hurts himself?"

Mr. Chessler crossed his arms. "I suppose you could refuse my offer. But that means you would forfeit."

Naturally, Mr. Spirro could surrender. But he didn't want to admit there was a small, quiet part of him that was excited in the revival of this game both he and Mr. Chessler had invented. The thrill of it invigorated him once more. He wasn't willing to part with that indescribable feeling of whimsy and charm just yet.

Before another moment of hesitation, Mr. Spirro straightened from the bench and offered Mr. Chessler a look of approval. It was then he began the short journey across the pathway and over toward the middle-aged man with the cane. As he meandered over, he thought that this could quite possibly be the very last time he and Mr. Chessler were together. After all, old age had finally claimed the both of them and it was already more than obvious that Mr. Chessler was deteriorating day by day, hour by hour. Naturally, there was every possibility the dear man would find rest and relaxation if he accepted his family's instructions to live in Norway for a while. However, Mr. Spirro wasn't entirely convinced that Mr. Chessler would ever return. The poor thing was already a shadow of his former self, and it made Mr. Spirro pity him.

Mr. Spirro thought of how today had probably been one of the few days when Mr. Chessler was truly and completely happy. After all, Mr. Chessler didn't seem like the type of person who was regularly content. Mr. Spirro imagined that much of the man's life was sequestered to solitary confinement. However, Mr. Chessler had seemed to glow when he first returned from his interaction with the old woman. He glimmered cheerfully in a way that Mr. Spirro had never seen before. The dear man was truly happy. How could Mr. Spirro fault him for that?

After a few moments, Mr. Spirro came upon the seated middle-aged man, the darkness of Mr. Spirro's shadow bleeding across the stranger so dramatically that it caused the man to look up and see what had blotted out most of the sunlight.

"I hope you'll excuse me," Mr. Spirro said. "I saw you from across the way and I thought I recognized you for a moment."

"Oh?" the middle-aged man said, straightening in his seat a little as if genuinely curious.

Mr. Spirro watched as the man squinted at him, studying his form, and assessing whether or not he knew him.

"I apologize for disturbing you," Mr. Spirro told him. "You looked so familiar, and I desperately wanted to introduce myself."

The man nodded politely. "That's very kind of you. You're more than welcome to sit down."

Mr. Spirro glanced back at Mr. Chessler observing them from across the causeway. Then his attention returned to the man.

"Thank you," he said to him. "I think I will for a moment. The afternoon sun is making me so tired."

"I'm more than happy to move, if you'd like," the man offered. "That way, you can spread out and enjoy yourself."

"Don't be silly, dear boy," Mr. Spirro told him, waving him off. "Then I wouldn't have the pleasure of your fine company."

The man smirked, chuckling a little. Mr. Spirro immediately took note.

"What's funny?" he asked. "Did I say something?"

"No. It's nothing. It's just—I haven't been referred to as a 'boy' in years," the man said, gripping the silver handle of his cane. "I don't feel much like one when I have to use this damn thing every day."

"A recent injury?" Mr. Spirro asked, eyeing the man's leg.

"Doctors say it will heal eventually," the man told him. "Just a few more months of physical therapy."

"How did it happen?" Mr. Spirro asked. "If you don't mind my asking?"

"I got drunk one night with some friends I knew in college," the man told him. "I guess it comes down to the fact that I'm not young anymore... I can't do the things that I used to do so freely and without consequence."

Mr. Spirro softened a little. He knew all about that. He knew first-hand how there's an invisible expiration date inscribed in each person and how things begin to fall apart before you're fully prepared.

The man glanced at Mr. Spirro, and it was then Mr. Spirro realized his attention had momentarily drifted away.

"I suppose you're going to tell me it's not true," the man said. "You'll tell me that age is just a number. It doesn't mean anything."

Mr. Spirro thought before answering. Of course, he could lie and make the man feel better. Or he could tell him the truth.

"No," he said. "I'm not going to tell you that."

Mr. Spirro noticed how the man seemed to recoil, perhaps shocked a little by his bluntness.

"I could tell you how your skin won't loosen, or certain body parts won't lose their firmness," Mr. Spirro told him. "But I'd be lying to you. The horrible truth is—people treat you differently once you're past a certain age. You become an affliction, a nuisance. You soil yourself. Your hair begins to thin. Your teeth fall away. It feels like evolution in reverse."

Mr. Spirro let the words linger in the balmy summertime air for a moment and eventually turned to face the man, realizing the poor thing's attention was glued to him with the same sort of bewildered look that children give their parents when they're unfairly chastised.

"I'm sorry, dear boy," Mr. Spirro said to the man. "You'll have to excuse my frankness. It must be the summer heat. I'm not usually so honest."

The man was quiet.

Mr. Spirro hoped he might respond—might say something, anything—but the man merely looked away, his attention drifting to the children playing on the grass nearby while their parents idled and gossiped.

Mr. Spirro stirred in his seat, remembering the reason why he had come over here in the first place. He eyed the man's cane, planning his assignment.

"I'm afraid I've overstayed my welcome," Mr. Spirro told him. "I hope you'll pardon my intrusion."

Once again, the man made no comment, his attention very much elsewhere.

It was then Mr. Spirro grabbed hold of the man's cane, as if bracing himself for support, and straightened from the bench. Finally, the moment he had been plotting and planning came to fruition. CRACK. The cane snapped under the pressure of Mr. Spirro's weight and sent him toppling down, crashing into the middle-aged man.

"What happened?" the man asked him.

"Oh, you'll have to pardon me," Mr. Spirro said, collecting himself. "I felt a little lightheaded and I grabbed your cane for support."

The man glanced down and noticed how his cane had been snapped in half.

"I'm so very sorry," Mr. Spirro said.

The man's eyes remained glued to his cane, going over and over the broken bits as if planning how he could make every effort to put them back together.

"Please forgive me, dear boy," Mr. Spirro told him. "It was a horrible accident. I should have never used your cane for support. I'm afraid I'm heavier than I think I am."

The man's eyes lowered, and he spoke softly. "At least you weren't hurt."

Mr. Spirro finally relaxed, realizing the man wouldn't fly off the handle as he had expected he might.

"Very kind of you to say," Mr. Spirro told him. "Please excuse me, won't you?"

Before the man could respond, Mr. Spirro lurched off the bench and began making his way back toward the bench where Mr. Chessler was seated, at the opposite end of the causeway. As he walked, he occasionally glanced over his shoulder and took note of the man as he mourned the loss of his cane. It wasn't long before the man swiped the broken pieces from the ground, lurched from his seat, and began limping away. For a moment, Mr. Spirro felt a sense of guilt for what he had done—the agony he had inflicted on that poor, unsuspecting stranger just for the sake of a game.

He watched in silence as the man staggered down the path in the other direction until he was out of view. Mr. Spirro felt a familiar pang in the center of his chest—a feeling of guilt and pity that seemed to spread to the furthest corners of his body. But before he could do anything about it, he heard Mr. Chessler calling to him and imploring him to hurry up.

Finally, Mr. Spirro arrived at the bench where his friend was seated. Mr. Chessler greeted him with warmness and affection, as usual.

"Splendid," Mr. Chessler told him. "I saw the whole thing. You were magnificent, of course. Not as rusty as I was with the old woman."

Mr. Spirro forced a polite smile. "I suppose I should probably go soon."

"What?" Mr. Chessler said, shocked and dismayed at the thought of Mr. Spirro abandoning him. "You can't leave yet. We're tied at the moment. We need to play another round to decide the winner."

But Mr. Spirro shook his head, waving Mr. Chessler away. "I'm too tired to keep playing."

"Nonsense," Mr. Chessler said, grabbing hold of Mr. Spirro's arm. "You have to play until we're finished."

For the very first time, Mr. Spirro felt a sense of fear for what he had created with Mr. Chessler. He was trapped. He knew for certain there wasn't much he could do to maneuver out of the situation without upsetting his friend. After all, he knew this would most likely be the very last time the two of them were ever together. Mr. Chessler would probably be sent away again and would perish while living abroad. And what then? Mr. Spirro would have soiled the memory of his friend by leaving him on such poor terms. He couldn't live with himself knowing he had upset Mr. Chessler, especially since the poor man felt some kind of romantic attachment to him.

"What shall the final round be?" Mr. Spirro asked him, imitating a smile.

He watched in silence as Mr. Chessler's attention drifted from one end of the park to the other. It was then he noticed how Mr. Chessler seemed to fix his attention quite naturally on a pair of mothers chatting near the edge of the riverbank, their children playing with one another in the grass nearby. One of the mothers regularly attended to a small infant curled inside a pink-colored pram with bits of paper cut in the shapes of stars and hearts threaded and dangling from the handlebars.

"An idea," Mr. Chessler told Mr. Spirro, grinning at him.

"Yes?"

"I want you to go over the riverbank and find a small pebble," Mr. Chessler told him. "When you've found it, I want you to go over to the pram. When the mother's not looking, I want you to feed the pebble to the baby."

Mr. Spirro could hardly believe what his friend was saying. It was too impossible, too disgusting to even consider. Of course, it was one thing to ruin the day of an elderly woman or a middle-aged man with a limp; however, it was something entirely different to bring agony upon a poor, defenseless child.

"You can't be serious," Mr. Spirro told him. "That's too... *sickening* to even consider."

"Then you forfeit?" Mr. Chessler asked.

"It's a ludicrous assignment. Consider something else."

"I'll do it," Mr. Chessler told him.

Mr. Spirro sensed himself recoil a little, shocked by his friend's admission. The thought that he could commit something so reprehensible, so vile, nearly made his stomach churn.

"Think of something else," Mr. Spirro begged him. "I won't do it."

"I know you won't," Mr. Chessler told him.

Before Mr. Spirro could utter another word, Mr. Chessler was already up, off the bench, and marching over toward the edge of the riverbank near where the group of middle-aged mothers had gathered to chat. Mr. Spirro thought of lunging after Mr. Chessler—doing anything to stop him, prevent him from going through with the horrible ordeal—but, more than anything, he didn't want to bring too much attention to himself. After all, Mr. Spirro conceded there was every possibility that Mr. Chessler wouldn't go through with the damn thing. Mr. Spirro clung to every invisible thread of hope that Mr. Chessler would lose his nerve and wouldn't be able to perform.

Mr. Spirro watched silently as Mr. Chessler knelt beside the riverbank and began to comb through the bed of rocks and pebbles that had washed ashore. Watching him carefully go through each and every possible option was nearly unbearable for Mr. Spirro. Moreover, it felt so decidedly ghoulish to observe Mr. Chessler while he searched for the proper stone to use to hurt the small child. But Mr. Spirro figured there was nothing he could do. After all, Mr. Chessler had already made up his mind and would be winning this game of *Prickle* whether Mr. Spirro liked it or not.

Finally, Mr. Chessler located a pebble that was to his liking—a small, round stone no bigger than a quarter.

Mr. Spirro observed as Mr. Chessler scaled the embankment where he had been kneeling and slowly approached the unsuspecting mothers and the child lying asleep in the pram. He maneuvered near them as stealthily as he could, skirting around the edge of the riverbank and coming upon the small pram while they had their backs turned.

Mr. Spirro sensed his stomach leap into his throat as he watched Mr. Chessler peer inside the pram and observe the sleeping baby.

What can I do? he wondered to himself. *Surely we've reached a point in this ridiculous affair where if I say something, he'll be caught and reprimanded.*

Mr. Spirro thought the only proper thing he could do would be to wait for Mr. Chessler to finish his business and pray to God that he won't be caught.

Mr. Chessler lifted the covering of the pram, exposing the infant. The small child stirred gently, stretching its arms. It was then that Mr. Spirro wondered if he saw Mr. Chessler hesitate slightly—if perhaps the very sight of the child might cause him to run away or, at the very least, think twice about what he was about to do. But no such luck. Mr. Chessler seemed to be invigorated by the sight of the cooing infant—all the possibilities of torture he could inflict upon the poor, helpless thing.

Before he could hesitate again, Mr. Chessler pushed the small pebble between the child's elastic-band lips. At first, there was silence. But then the child began to resist slightly, struggling against Mr. Chessler's force as he continued to try to pry open the infant's lips and slide the pebble inside its tiny mouth.

The child began to cry.

Mr. Chessler lurched back, surprised at the loudness of the infant's shrieks. It was then that the nearby mothers turned and saw what Mr. Chessler was attempting to do. They shouted at him, starting to approach.

Mr. Spirro straightened from the bench, preparing to intervene but also somewhat hesitant to get involved in case things became truly difficult.

Just then, in a moment that seemed to happen in slow-motion, Mr. Chessler snatched the shrieking infant from the pram and hurled the poor thing into the river.

Mr. Spirro sensed his eyes widen with horror, trying to make sense of what he had just seen. *Has Mr. Chessler really just done that?* he thought to himself. *Surely, that can't be possible.*

But it was true. It had happened.

Mr. Spirro observed without comment as the mothers rushed toward Mr. Chessler at the pram and seemed to stop short as soon as he flung the child into the river. One of the mothers screamed and dove into the water, swimming after the poor child. It was no use, however. The child's body had already slipped beneath the water's oily black surface, sinking to the bottom of the river as if it were tethered to concrete weights.

A crowd began to gather around the scene, some of the women shouting for Mr. Chessler to be restrained. Several men came forward and took hold of him while the old man fell to his knees, laughing. It was the hearty, emphatic laugh of a madman—the horrible kind of laugh that reached deep inside Mr. Spirro and twisted his guts into ribbons while prickling the hairs on the nape of his neck.

ACKNOWLEDGMENTS

Of course, the creation of any book does not occur inside a vacuum. There are countless kind souls to whom I'm indebted for guiding me as I steadily worked on this collection of stories.

I'm especially grateful for the tenderness and care of my literary agent, Priya Doraswamy. Priya was instrumental in the design and the development of these tales. I'd also like to extend similar gratitude to my Film/TV Manager, Ryan Lewis. Ryan assisted me quite a bit during the creation of this book and truly helped improve the quality of these stories.

I send all my love and gratitude to my brilliant editor Cath Trechman. I owe Cath a great deal for her support, generosity, and kindness. To that end, I must thank the entire Titan team. It has been truly so wonderful to work with such dedicated and talented people. I hope there are many more books in our future.

Finally, I extend all my thanks to you, dear reader. I realize these stories might be upsetting for some, so I sincerely thank you for approaching this book with the sensitivity and care that it requires.

ABOUT THE AUTHOR

ERIC LAROCCA (*he/they*) is a 2x Bram Stoker Award® finalist and Splatterpunk Award winner. Named by *Esquire* as one of the "Writers Shaping Horror's Next Golden Age" and praised by *Locus* a "one of the strongest and most unique voices in contemporary horror fiction," LaRocca's notable works include *Things Have Goteen Worse Since We Last Spoke*, *Everything the Darkness Eats*, *The Trees Grew Because I Bled There: Collected Stories*, and his latest work *At Dark, I Become Loathsome*. A lover of luxury fashion and an admirer of European musical theatre, Eric can often be found roaming the streets of his home city, Boston, MA, for inspiration. For more information, please visit ericlarocca.com.

THINGS HAVE GOTTEN WORSE SINCE WE LAST SPOKE AND OTHER MISFORTUNES

Eric LaRocca

A whirlpool of darkness churns at the heart of a macabre ballet between two lonely young women in an internet chat room in the early 2000s—a darkness that threatens to forever transform them once they finally succumb to their most horrific desires.

A couple isolate themselves on a remote island in an attempt to recover from their teenage son's death, when a mysterious young man knocks on their door...

And a man confronts his neighbour when he discovers a strange object in his back yard, only to be drawn into an ever-more dangerous game.

Three devastating, beautifully written horror stories from one of the genre's most cutting-edge voices.

"Some horror walks you down a dark corridor, where there's whispers and laughter, sobs and screams. Other horror starts down at the end of that corridor, where there's a door that opens on to you don't know what. Read this, and then decide where Eric LaRocca has left you. Not that it matters. There's no way out."

Stephen Graham Jones, author of *The Only Good Indians* and *My Heart is a Chainsaw*

"Eric LaRocca's unflinching *Things Have Gotten Worse Since We Last Spoke* will crawl inside you, move stuff around, and make you see the world differently, like all great stories do."

Paul Tremblay, author of *A Head Full of Ghosts* and *The Pallbearers Club*

TITANBOOKS.COM

THE TREES GREW BECAUSE I BLED THERE: COLLECTED STORIES

Eric LaRocca

Eight stories of literary dark fiction from a master storyteller. Exploring the shadow side of love, these are tales of grief, obsession, control. Intricate examinations of trauma and tragedy in raw, poetic prose. In these narratives, a woman imagines horrific scenarios whilst caring for her infant niece; on-line posts chronicle a cancer diagnosis; a couple in the park with their small child encounter a stranger with horrific consequences; a toxic relationship reaches a terrifying resolution…

A beautifully crafted, devastating short fiction collection from the Bram Stoker Awards® finalist and author of *Things Have Gotten Worse Since We Last Spoke and Other Misfortunes*.

"The stories collected here are by turns confident, brutal, and breathtaking… must-read horror."

The New York Times

"These stories are body horror at its best—but they also enter the realms of dark relationships, intrusions that change our lives forever, obviously not for the best, the fear of illness, of taking care, of love, of obsession, of attachment. They are nightmarish and they are deeply human. I loved them and also my jaw dropped at how daring they are, how far they go. Eric LaRocca is not only good: there's courage in his literature."

Mariana Enriquez, author of *Our Share of Night*

TITANBOOKS.COM

For more fantastic fiction, author events,
exclusive excerpts, competitions, limited editions and more

VISIT OUR WEBSITE
titanbooks.com

LIKE US ON FACEBOOK
facebook.com/titanbooks

FOLLOW US ON TWITTER AND INSTAGRAM
@TitanBooks

EMAIL US
readerfeedback@titanemail.com